STRANGE WONDERS

WONDERS

A COLLECTION OF RARE **FRITZ**

LEIBER WORKS

STRANGE
WONDERS
A COLLECTION OF RARE FRITZ
LEIBER WORKS

Edited by
BENJAMIN SZUMSKYJ

SUBTERRANEAN PRESS 2010

Original Sources for Reprinted Material—

❖ "Challenge" originally appeared in *The Acolyte* #9
   (Winter 1945)
❖ "Demons of the Upper Air" was first published as a booklet
   by Roy A. Squires (1969)
❖ "Ghosts" originally appeared in *The Acolyte* #9 (Winter 1945)
❖ "The Gray Mouser I" & "The Gray Mouser II" originally appeared
   in The *Acolyte* #8 (Fall 1944)
❖ *The Mystery of the Japanese Clock* (Montgolfier Press, 1982)
❖ "Night of Death" appeared in *Myrddin* #2 (August 1975)
❖ *Quicks around the Zodiac—A Farce* (Cheap Street Press, 1983)
❖ "Recognition of Death" originally appeared in *The Acolyte* #10
   (Spring 1945)
❖ "The Tale of the Grain Ships: A Fragment," originally appeared in
   The New York Review of Science Fiction (May 1997)
❖ "Introduction," "Adventures of a Balloon," "Further Adventures
   of a Balloon," "Riches and Power," "Children of Jerusalem," "The
   Road to Jordan" and "After the Darkness" appeared *In the Beginning*
   (Cheap Street Press, 1983)
❖ "Past Druid Guards," "Santa Monica Beach at Sunset," "1959: the
   Beach at Santa Monica," "The Midnight Wall," "5447 Ridgewood
   Court," "The Other Side," "Poor Little Ape," and "The Voice of
   Man" originally appeared in *Sonnets to Jonquil and All* (Roy A.
   Squires, 1978)

First Edition

ISBN 978-1-59606-324-2

Subterranean Press
PO Box 190106
Burton, MI 48519

www.subterraneanpress.com

TABLE OF CONTENTS

IN THE BEGINNING

POETRY BY FRITZ LEIBER

OTHER WORKS BY FRITZ LEIBER

Acknowledgements–

I would like to thank the following people for their help in making this publication come true. First, I would like to thank Richard Curtis, whose faith in me is something that I will not forget and I look forward to working with him in the future. Justin Leiber, for providing me with many insights on his father's life and works. Bruce Byfield, for writing *Witches of the Mind: A Critical Study of Fritz Leiber* and being so helpful and generous with me and my travails. I am indeed grateful to many of my friends and colleagues—S. T. Joshi, John Howard, the staff at DreamHaven Books, A. Langley Searles, Julie Grob of the Special Collections Department at the University of Houston, John Pelan, Martin Andersson, and Phillip A. Ellis. Lastly, I would like to thank all past and present members of S.S.W.F.T., for both supporting and publishing my dreams.

Dedicated to Bruce Byfield & Justin Leiber

THE CREAM OF THE DAMNED
An Introduction

WHEN THE WORLD of literature mourns an author, such as Fritz Reuter Leiber Jr. (1910–1992), one of the many thoughts racing through the minds of family, friend and fan alike, is whether the author in question left behind a plethora of unpublished fiction. This thought is not necessarily triggered by motivations of financial profit; rather, admirers are often curious as to what was left *out* of the published corpus of their work. The act of canonization often has readers wondering this. Usually, there is a sound reason for the author to have kept such works under lock and key: they are drafts of work in progress, juvenilia, addenda, practice, random writings, unusable, or simply they are too weak in either characterization or plot to have been deemed worthy of publication. Ironically, however, they are not destroyed by the author, as if they have been deemed too precious to place within the author's already full wastebasket. As such, it seems likely that the authors know that one day, many years after their death, someone is likely to find this material…and it is that individual's decision, then, to either ensure it remains unpublished *or* make it available to readers new and old alike.

BENJAMIN SZUMSKYJ

In the field of literature, there have been discussions as to whether it is appropriate to publish the works of a dead author. Some see it as distasteful, with the author sure to dismiss such an action if alive and well. For example, before their deaths, authors as diverse as Kafka, Hardy and Virgil wanted their unpublished works to be destroyed after their deaths. We have also seen incomplete works published, such as Dickens' *The Mystery of Edwin Drood* and Poe's "The Lighthouse." This is a fair enough statement. Yet, we are to never know, if there are no specific instructions left by the author in question. And again, in not destroying them themselves, and in keeping them, the author has already subconsciously preserved them, and allowed the possibility of their postmortem unearthing. Many welcome the publication of such material, as in doing so we may learn a great deal more about the author whom we admire, unlocking in turn new perspectives of that individual.

In regards to Fritz Leiber, I believe that publication of such works only strengthens his literary greatness. Through fragments, drafts and practice writings, we can clearly see the evolution from Leiber, the amateur, to Leiber, the professional. We are exposed to the clear way in which he dedicated his life to the written word and trained his abilities to produce the award-winning masterpieces that we read even today. While some may object to such a volume, I ask them this—is not the dream just as important as the empire that had been built from it? Are not the blueprints and sketches as impressive as the buildings and the artwork? We must place all this into perspective, and see that publishing such works is not a smear upon Leiber's legacy. Rather, it completes a full circle. If we are asked to be thorough in the biography of an individual, then we must also do so for their bibliography.

Leiber is a name, of course, that has earned respect and overwhelming appreciation for over half a century. Fritz Leiber, Sr. and his wife, Virginia, a romanticised meeting between Shakespeare and Queen Titania if I have ever heard one, gave birth to Fritz Jr. in the years leading up to what would be termed the Great War. His very individual seemingly moulded by the hands of Shakespeare, Robert Graves, Jung, and he was destined to find a literary guardian in H. P. Lovecraft, friends Harry O. Fischer and Franklin MacKnight, and his two loves and companions, Jonquil Stephens and Margo Skinner. It was inevitable that Leiber was going to stand forth from the crowd, and to establish his name in some avenue of art. Fritz Leiber is a unique writer; he draws from so many different inspirations, whether it be his personal life— explored with unusual candour in his novels, as well as in his saga of Fafhrd and the Gray Mouser—or his literary or philosophical influences, showcased again in any one of his brilliant novels.

This volume is divided into four distinct areas. The first concerns Leiber's fragments, drafts and miscellanea. The second section re-publishes the contents of the rare volume *In the Beginning*. The third section contains all of Leiber's known poetry, a form of his writing many have been unaware of. The final section re-publishes the rare works *The Mystery of the Japanese Clocks* and *Quicks around the Zodiac—A Farce*.

Some history is required to fully appreciate the contents of this volume. First, we are lucky to even *have* the following unpublished material. Believe it or not, the material was almost lost in a computer crash: technology can be a cruel mistress. Fortunately, it survived, because it had been sent to Richard Curtis' office earlier that week. The folder containing this material was then given to Bruce Byfield, Fritz Leiber

scholar and author of *Witches of the Mind: A Critical Study
of Fritz Leiber*, by Justin Leiber shortly after Leiber's death in
1992. Byfield believes that most of the material was probably written between 1937 and about 1948, although several
pieces may have been written later. Most of the material is
printed on cheap typing paper, and is in fragile condition; its
survival was as tenuous as its physical condition. Some pieces
are unpublished practice works. At the time, Leiber was trying
to discipline himself to write daily, and to extend his range of
writing. If you look at the notes he made about the rationale
for these exercises, one might be able to gain some insight into
Leiber's working methods.

The longer pieces, mostly titled, are short stories or
opening chapters of novels. Most of these seem to date
from the 1940s, and several can be related directly to what
Leiber actually published during that time, or to events in his
own life. The jewel among this material is "The Tale of the
Grain Ships," which dates to 1936-37, for which we also have
numerous notes. Leiber mentions the planned novel in several
places, and Bruce Byfield notes the following:

> "['The Tale of the Grain Ships"] is from the
> manuscript which eventually became the first sec-
> tion of *The Swords of Lankhmar*. Written in 1937, it
> is heavily influenced by Robert Graves' novels about
> the Roman emperor Claudius, which were among
> Leiber's lifetime favorites. This influence is especially
> obvious in the characterization of Claudius, although
> Leiber, viewing the emperor from the outside, pro-
> vides a livelier depiction than Graves' pseudo-
> autobiographies. When the fragment was written,
> Fafhrd and the Gray Mouser were heroes who were

constantly reincarnated throughout Earth's history, Ningauble was an immortal sorcerer, and Sheelba was not invented yet. 'Adept's Gambit,' originally shared the same background. I might also add that the modern language—so different from 'Adept's Gambit' is another sign of Graves' influence on the fragment. Also, the bundle of material contains unorganized notes about the rest of the story. It seemed to have included plans for an early barbarian invasion. In his columns for *Fantasy Newsletter*, Fritz refers to it several times. He seems to have believed that the story was far too complex and ambitious for the writing skills he possessed when he started writing it."

Justin Leiber knew little about the material, but, from internal evidence and Byfield's knowledge of Fritz's life, one can make a few brief comments and guesses about some of the pieces. Bruce Byfield has also provided me with the following information.

"The Communicants" seems similar in style and subject to *Gather, Darkness!* so it is believed that it dates from the mid-1940s, when Fritz was trying to crack the science fiction market after achieving some success as a fantasist. With its emphasis on the outcast, it probably came after *Gather, Darkness!*, when this theme starts to enter his work (as in "You're All Alone").

"The Feeler" probably dates to the late 1940s. The acknowledgement suggests that he had discovered fandom by this point, and some of the writing is reminiscent of "Poor Superman." Leiber notes that the story is "based on ideas given me by Judith Merril and Katherine MacLean."

"Insanity" is another piece from the late 1940s, judging from the title and the "Poor Superman"-like names and background. This belief also comes from the title, because in this period Fritz used a number of one-word titles that related to an emotion or psychological state, rather like Jane Austen.

The background to "Lesher" seems based on Fritz's efforts to write for encyclopedias in the 1940s. The closeness of the name "Lesher" to "Leiber" further supports this idea, although the name may also be adapted from the Leshy in James Branch Cabell's works.

"The Adventurer," from the style, seems much later than any of the other pieces in the folder. It may be as late as the 1960s or 1970s. If one remembers "Not Much Disorder and Not So Early Sex," Fritz noted that "Black Glass" is another story in which early childhood imaginings played a part.

"Opaque Corridor" is reminiscent of a story in "The Mind Spider," possibly with the same psychiatrist as a hero. The story is sometimes called "Serenity Shoals," Byfield believes. That similarity suggests the early 1950s for this fragment.

"Predator Universe" sounds like "You're All Alone," so the late 1940s seems the best guess for its origin. Again, there's a background of an encyclopedia office and the very title suggests the drama of A. E. van Vogt.

"The Social Inventor" is another probably from the late 1940s, although it could have been written as much as ten years after that. It is almost a complete draft, with the main ideas fleshed out, but characterization and plot development not fully realized.

There is not much certain about "Trap," but its style suggests it was written around 1950.

"The Wrong Track" is very autobiographical in nature. Obviously taking place during World War II, it seems to draw on Fritz's experiences working for Douglas Aircraft instead of registering as a conscientious objector. The tension he felt at the time about his guilt in neither fighting nor registering as a conscientious objector would eventually lead to several years in the mid 1940s when he had trouble writing. There may also be a depiction of his home-life with his first wife.

"Concerning Tribalism and Loving the World" is probably an attempt to practice writing daily. The title and contents suggests Fritz's *New Purposes* magazine. Beneath the high-sounding rhetoric, there may be, like so much of *New Purposes*, an elaborate justification for free love and other aspects of bohemian or beat culture, as the rather shy and diffident Leiber tried to nerve himself to explore them.

The fragment for "The Red-Headed Nightmare" is a title of a novel that Fritz tried to write for a couple of years, possibly in the early 1950s, but this is unconfirmed. The first couple of pages show a quiet liberal's view of the Cold War. According to Stephensen-Payne and Benson Jr. in their bibliography *Fritz Leiber: Sardonic Swordsman—Part 2* (1990, p. 81) this title was "used both for an unfinished detective novel about a group of Chicago alcoholics and for a projected sf novel," no doubt reflecting in part, Leiber's own experiences.

"Notes for a Study of Mac" and "Mac" are the notes for a piece of practice writing and the actual result. So far as I know, this is the first and only piece of Fritz's work in which we have complete working notes and the finished result. Among other things, it shows Fritz as a systematic outliner, setting down everything he wanted to say before starting to write. Perhaps this approach freed him to focus on style when he finally wrote. It might also explain his relatively unprolific output. Compared to the romanticized depictions of Harry Fischer, the portrayal of Mac seems an effort at clear-headed observation. It's interesting that Fritz's two lifelong male friendships were so opposite: one based on fantasy with little knowledge of reality (Fischer) and one based on analysis and the give and take of discussion by letter.

Of the re-published material, little more can be added to that which has already been said and documented by past essayists, reviewers and introducers. Of the little more than a dozen of Leiber's poems that are still existent, all showcase a wide diversity of themes and topics. Most appeared in *Sonnets to Jonquil and All*, for which he also wrote an afterword. Many use free verse to convey his particular worldview. "Ghosts," for example, echoes the modernization of the supernatural, which would become a key trait of Leiber's short stories, as does the haunting "Night of Death." The Howardian "Challenge" appears to speak of a converted Christian mercenary who's decide to cease killing for Satan's pleasure, whilst "Past Druid Guards" chronicles the activities of the mystic clan who "past our bower's quivering scrim…see / The galloping mirthless hordes of destiny." The latter was written during Leiber's time as an undergraduate at the University of Chicago. In contrast, "The Recognition of Death" narrates death's advocate, who respects and is befriended by the figure of bereavement. Both "Santa Monica Beach at Sunset" and "1959: the Beach at Santa Monica" speak of the fragility of life and the potency of a locale that may have been germinal to Leiber. Interestingly, Leiber comments that "Santa Monica Beach at Sunset" in "tertrameter [sic] echoes another war, Vietnam." "The Midnight Wall", "5447 Ridgewood Court" (where Leiber lived for twelve years) and "The Other Side" are all heartfelt, brutal and elegiac sonnets on Jonquil E. Stephens, months after her untimely death. Emotion soaks each and every of their lines. The amusing "Poor Little Ape" first appeared in Leiber's novel *The Wanderer*, while "The Voice of Man" is a pessimistic depiction of mankind who voices "the very heart of solitude." Both of these were composed while Leiber "was working as a precision inspector at Douglas Aircraft in Santa Monica during World War II." "The Demons of the Upper Air" is in eight sections; it veers between passages of free verse, and passages of loosely rendered formalist verse, giving several perspectives on the eponymous demons, some from their own perspective. It is a detailed account of the bond shared between demons and humanity, fear, and the double-nature of all things.

There appears to be two versions of "The Gray Mouser," "The Gray Mouser I" and "The Gray Mouser II," both being quaint and fitting stanzas on the second half of Lankhmar's dynamic duo, peppered with Leiber trademark idiolect. The first comes from the magazine *The Acolyte* (which has been used here) and the second, from *Sonnets to Jonquil and All* (which has been slighty edited, presumably, by Roy A. Squires). That Leiber did not write any poetry for Fafhrd, a fictionalised version of himself (except, of course, for some of the impromptu poetry he recites in *Swords Against Death*— Fafhrd being the one with bardic training, who makes songs rather than sings them) indicates that the poems were written to honor his friend Harry Otto Fischer, who is fictionally represented by the Gray Mouser. "The Gray Mouser I" is a glorification of the Mouser's trade and thieving abilities, while "The Gray Mouser II" boasts that even the most feared and impenetrable of Lankhmar's buildings, is no match for the craftiness of the mockful Gray Mouser.

Leiber's own words will introduce the section entitled *In the Beginning*, later in the volume, but it can be said that these beautiful children's stories were originally written for the religious journal, *The Churchman*, in the summer of 1934. Maybe, mention should be made that Leiber flirted with religion shortly before this, and wrote them for the clergyman who had sponsored his admission into the seminary, possibly feeling that he owed him something. *The Mystery of the Japanese Clock* is mentioned in the eighth part of Leiber's autobiographical essay "My Life and Writings," and it details the deconstruction of a digital clock with great depth, while *Quicks around the Zodiac—A Farce* is a cosmic comedy revolving around the saga of the Quick Family and their encounters with the house of the zodiac.

Fritz Leiber—man, myth and legend—is an author who must be studied in the light of his vast talents and abilities over so many genres, as one whose writings do not merely entertain or pay the bills, but which contribute to the field, setting a standard, and featuring stories that contain a depth and substance transcending much that came before, during, and after his own lifetime. As the title of this introduction suggests, despite his alcoholism, guilt over his wife and his melancholy and loneliness, Leiber managed to produce memorable works of fiction. By printing these rare works, particularly the unpublished material, we learn a great deal more of the growth of one of America's great authors. Fritz Leiber, as his literary executor Richard Curtis once said to me, "is a vintage wine to connoisseurs. He matures with age and gets better and better." I couldn't agree with him more.

Benjamin Szumskyj, Editor
Melville, Western Australia—2008

FRAGMENTS,
DRAFTS AND
MISCELLANEA

THE TALE OF THE GRAIN SHIPS—

A FRAGMENT

COVERED WITH SWEAT and filth, Xikses of Crete, known to a very few as The Gray Mouser, wriggled his way upward. His mouth and nose curled in half-humorous disgust at the stenches filtering up from behind. There was no getting used to those stenches; they had too much variety.

By now he ought to be seeing light ahead, yet did not. Only too easy to have taken a wrong turning in the mucky road behind. But he'd see himself in Parthia, he thought, before he'd turn back. Whatever kitchen or bath he ended up in he'd brazen it out.

Bath? He'd be drowned for sure if a lot of water came atop him now. For a moment he braced his barked elbows against the rounded sides and paused in fearful doubt. Then he realized that the pipe he was in was dry as dust, disused for some time, at least. He couldn't laugh much for panting and sneezing, but tried to and then continued on his way.

In a little while the pipe suddenly turned upward. Had one of those lazy slaves gotten energetic and put the cover back on? That was his only chance of being right. He straightened up, hands above head, in the new section of pipe and chuckled relievedly as he touched a top, a metallic top. Bracing himself carefully against a slip, he pushed it easily upward, welcoming the air of the upper surface.

Pig-ears, assistant to the alternate cook's helper, dozing, ruminated the hot hours away in the old garden, now not used except for the raising of a few imported vegetable delicacies. He dangled his great shanks over the edge of the old swimming pool and dreamed of a perpetual Saturnalia, with himself forever wearing the master's robe, and Freckles, the between-porticos maid, to wash his feet. Freckles just thought too much of herself the way it was now.

Still half in the dream-world, where all was possible, he unconcernedly saw the round cover of the drain lift slowly upward. It did not even bother him when he noted a black and brown smeared face studying him gravely from out the crescent of shadow. He had seen as bothersome things happen in many of his dreams. So he waited confidently for the drain-cover to turn into a warming plate and the head into a small roast.

When this did not happen as soon as it should have, he became vaguely annoyed. Unblinking eyes continued to regard him with a mild reproof. He felt himself filled with a nameless anxiety. The surroundings were becoming a little too real for a dream, and there was something very unpleasant about the stare of those eyes. He blinked his own a couple of times, but still the dream wouldn't go away. Rapidly the only dreamlike quality in the situation was becoming his own inability to move.

Then there came from beneath the drain-cover a dirty, naked arm, pointing directly at his belly.

"Pig-ears!" rumbled a deep voice, "I've come to take your stomach to the god of gluttony in hell. It's too bad, Pig-ears, but it eats too many stolen scraps. We want pretty stomachs. Come, Pig-ears, and let me remove it."

Pig-ears didn't stop to think that the drain-pipe would give any voice a sepulchral quality. He rolled over backwards rapidly.

"Help!" he squealed in the voice of his namesake, "Come here, somebody, come here, please!"

His appeal was answered by several kitchen and house slaves who were always ready for a bit of excitement. They were greeted by a vision of the tumbling Pig-ears and a sound of martial clangor from the old pool (the Mouser was beating the copper drain cover diligently against the stone). Just as the first of them almost reached the edge, the Mouser leapt catlike up and so appeared to them almost as by magic.

Immediately on landing, he struck a heroic attitude, simultaneously kicking the first cook in the stomach. The others paused: there was something arresting in the short, brown, dirt-covered figure clad only in a loin cloth.

Besides, it looked to them as if the cook had gone down on his knees of his own accord.

"Fly for your lives," cried the Mouser in a hysterical voice. "The Parthians have crossed the Mediterranean in a fleet of baskets! Even now they are upon Rome! The Guards are in route! I had to come through the sewers to pass the enemy line."

It happened that Asiaticus and a couple of other senators had been booming, for political reasons, the ridiculous possibility of a Parthian invasion of the eastern empire. So, when the Mouser threw up one elbow and tragically covered one eye, the slaves were sufficiently in amaze to let him stalk through their ranks into the kitchen.

A few deep breaths recovered all of them, save the stomach-kicked cook, to their usually hardy incredulity, but, when they had angrily pursued the mysterious intruder, it was to find him jigging lightly around the sink with a giggling maid, artfully dodging the wild, swashing strokes of the head-cook's master-ladle, the whilst singing,

> "O, our slaves aren't slaves these modern days,
> They really rule the nation,
> They slide into their master's beds,
> They brow-beat men of station."

"Take it away! Take it away!" panted the cook in a squeaking voice with a thick eastern accent. "Already it almost upsets the stew."

Pig-ears peeked in through the door.

"I seen it first," he called out guardedly. "It's a Greek witch, it is. Better give it what it wants. Maybe it's after Freckles."

Still sang the Mouser,

> "Rich man's villa has a slave,
> A perfumed, bookish dandy;
> They gape at his philosophy
> The whilst he snitches candy."

And, suiting the action to the word, he picked, in passing, a couple of almonds from the sweatmeat-mosaiced meat-cake.

The head-cook screamed, a scullery boy automatically ran for the almond jar, and the under-cook who had been kicked managed to gasp out, "Come on, jump him, the dirty guttersnipe!"

"Your description is accurate," said the Mouser, as he calmly swung his sweating partner careening into the advancing motley phalanx. "But," he continued, skipping lightly away and up a set of wall shelves, "You forget one thing."

Clinging to the topmost shelf, he swung around and raised his hand, palm forward, in a gesture that his precarious position made the more impressive.

"Though a guttersnipe, I am a Roman citizen!" he thundered in the voice of a centurion. The broom, cleaver, and ladle-armed army stopped dead.

"Imagine this room the blood-splattered arena," he went on swiftly, taking advantage of the moment of silence that he had created. "It is near the end of a magnificent day. You are a group of gladiators who have survived an onslaught of Germans, Balerics, Africs, great-roaring lions, stone-hided monsters from the east, thousand toothed dog backs—so many that you cannot remember the first of them, but feel that you have warred continuously since a time when even Rome was not. See there, how great-paunch wipes the red sweat of carnage from his brow!"

The head-cook, startled but inwardly delighted at the martial description, smiled a little in […]

A couple of hard heads might have broken the Mouser's spell with one common sense remark, but he forestalled them with another burst.

"Your bodies are stiff, but your spirits as unbroken as Great Julius Caesar's or Great Guts Marcius. The crowd is delighted with you, deafens you with shouts of praise, rains upon you roses, golden coins, and seat covers. Even our good old Claudius stumbles to his feet and yells, 'Wwwwu…wu…wu…well ddd-d-done, you gg-gg—good fellows. I dd-do believe you should be set free, I dddd…ddd…dd-DO INDEED, my lords. In fact, I am reminded of the ff-fffaithful donkey who…of course, I dd-dd-don't meant that you're donkeys, I really dd-ddddddd-DON'T…'"

Here, the Mouser gave such a good imitation, rolling his eyes, weaving his head, stuttering, and slobbering, that, to maintain the suspense, he had to forestall a round of applause by changing the subject.

"But who is it that arises from the box next Caesar's? Who? A dark little senator—born in Spain, rot him—who sneers" (Here, the Mouser contorted his face into a fearful grimace) and says, "Such louts I never saw cheered. Give me a net and trident and I could beat any one of them myself. Rome is the home of two things: coward gladiators, and lousy cooks!"

Here, the cooks in the Mouser's audience snarled audibly. But all the kitchen fry hung on his words, in the inescapable grip of the illusion. To them, the arena was glamour incarnate. That it was forbidden to most of them, that only a lucky slave here or there had even glimpsed the bloody madness of the games, only stimulated their striding desire. Even those who could not write kept tallies of the number of men and beasts their favorites had killed; the scullery boys collected souvenirs (none of which were genuine), and a great deal of petty wagering went on. Pig-ears dreamt of becoming a gladiator; Freckles, of sleeping with one.

The Mouser shrank back into a shelf and whispered: "There is a sudden hush. Then comments and threats pass about like the hissing of snakes. Good old Claudius can only stutter at first, but finally manages to say to the little, sunburst Spanish dandy, 'Wwww-www…wu-wuwell, we're a frfrrr-fff-free ppp-pp-people, so I gg-guess you can say whu…what you want to, bb-bb-but even at that yy-you ought to pp… ppru-pppPROVE IT. Oughtn't he to, lads? I ggggu-gu-gu-guess we're not so miserly bb-but that there's an extra trident and net somewhere.'

"The Spaniard looks coldly at our Caesar" (Here the Mouser made his eyes as round and staring as a cat's), "and comes down to the edge of the wall."

The Mouser let himself down two shelves and the saucepan gladiators edged back with unconsciously appropriate threateningness. "An attendant gives him a net" (here, the Mouser flipped from behind him a lace tablecloth that was handy), "and points to a discarded trident at the foot of the wall" (indicating a large broom standing nearby).

Just then, the Mouser realized that he was using his control of the kitchen mob to increase their animosity rather than to save himself, but, as usual, he was too hypnotized by the mirror of his own polishing to modify in the least his course of action.

"What do you gladiators do?" he questioned, with a wide sweep of his hand, palm upward. "The honour of Rome is at stake, your honour, you blood-thirsty bastards.

"You mutter."

The kitchen slaves muttered.

"You look around."

The kitchen slaves look around.

"You must choose one from among you to best the sneering Spaniard. Of whom else could you think then but your champion, Great Paunch?"

The head-cook waved his ladle from sheer delight; those about him edged away, eying him enviously.

"He already has his sword gripped ready. One of you hands him that buckler there!"

A gaping scullery-boy put the pot cover that the Mouser was pointing at into the head-cook's hand. The head cook, gripping it by the handle, held it up in what he considered to be a most professional position.

"The Spaniard leaps down into the arena and—the fight is on!"

Here, the Mouser sprang lightly down, picked up the broom in passing, and rushed at the head cook, rather unsuccessfully swinging the tablecloth around his head. The rest stepped back, leaving standing alone Great Paunch, who pushed the pot cover out in front of him as if it were a wall, and raised the two foot long pewter ladle high above his head. The Mouser dodged to one side of its downward swipe and swung the table cloth around the head and arms of his adversary. He gave it a jerk, Great Paunch tottered, but, just at that moment, the Mouser's foot hit a grease spot, and he sat down suddenly and unintentionally.

Great Paunch, who was by no means a slow thinker, noticed this with the one eye uncovered by the blinding cloth and directed his own more ponderous and stately fall toward the one already fallen. The Mouser rolled out from under just in time, writhed sinuously to his feet, and, as his great opponent attempted to follow suit, poked him in the stomach with the broom.

"Thus dispose I of your greatest, O Romans," he cried, and, giving a bloodthirsty scream, sprang onto a table.

The others rushed at him in mass. He waited until they were almost upon him, then leapt, with some surprise, to the shoulders of the leader and, tripping lightly on head and collar bone, made swift way toward a door leading to the interior of the house.

One of those to the rear grabbed him by the ankle, but, as he slashed downward, he managed to grab the heavy curtain, designed to keep out kitchen odors, and so to jerk himself loose and out of the room before even his feet hit the ground. He slid, stayed himself by grasping an inner curtain, and rushed on, for the stew of underlings, forgetful with excitement, were overflowing their proper precinct in pursuit.

He ducked under the arms of a more showily caparisoned slave, played a few moments tag among the portico-pillars with the screaming van, then proceeded by but one fleet glance, darted through a door into the new gardens at the side of the house.

That fleeting glance had told him that there were congregated about the large pond, a group of people as excited and preoccupied as that at his heels. However, this group was fashionably dressed, and its excitement, although hysterical, was laughing rather than angry. A half dozen of the young ladies and matrons were holding an impromptu diving contest. There had been some joking about the haughty matron Agrippinila's experiences as a sponge diver while in exile, and so the thing had derisorily come about. Someone had thrown a silver goblet into the pond, and all the guests were crowded about, cheering and jibing, as the slightly drunken contestants plunged confusedly in.

The Mouser, seeing here his chance (since none of their eyes would be upon him), dashed a straight course toward the pool, and, skimming such a low course in his dive between a press of legs that he grazed the edge, was under water before any noticed that it wasn't just another of the girls.

At almost the same time, those about the pool became aware of the howling influx of kitchen slaves, who were still hot on the intruder's trail. Some of the guests paled and looked for a place to hide. After all, there had been some dangerous slave revolts in Rome within the last two centuries.

A black-haired Greek, magnificently dressed in red, with a sharp featured, worried face, jumped to his feet and shouted at the sweating, puffing kitchen fry.

"What's this mean? Get back with you, or I'll have you all lashed half to death. What's your reason for this?"

At the incisive sound of his voice, the leaders stopped dead; those that followed pushed and jostled them a few feet further before they realized what they had done and stopped, too. They all peered about in terror and in complete wonder as to how they had ever gotten into the forbidden precincts.

Then, as the garden slaves were advancing on them threateningly, the cook who had been kicked in the stomach got his tongue back and said hurriedly, "We were trying to protect you, Master, that's all. From a dirty, brown, murdersome little man, who was after your mastership's life, I'm sure. Even now, I saw him jump into the pond."

The divers, who had been watching the scene with dazed amusement while supporting themselves with their hands on the pond's stoned edge, made a great screaming and commotion, pushing one another back in their wild endeavor to get out and away from the unseen terror that they already imagined pawing at their feet.

"Rubbish," said an older man with serious face.

But just at that moment and in the midst of the churning, there emerged from the pool a masculine face, white-skinned, that reminded one irresistibly of a squat helmet.

"Posides," it said quickly in a cultured voice, "I almost got it just now. It's either a man or else a turbot that somebody sneaked into the pool.

At the word "turbot," the girls stayed their screaming and made good their escape in a moment. The one in the pool who had just spoken, waved jauntily at the others and then dived under again, disregarding the warnings that were shouted at him. For full twenty heartbeats he was under the muddy waters before reappearing.

"No sign of anything now," he said.

Pig-ears could not restrain himself at this.

"I seen it come up through the drain in the old pool," he said. "And now it's got away through the other. It said it was some sort of thing from the underworld, but I'll bet 'twas a Greek witch. They can make themselves anything, even a fish."

"Keep still, all of you, and go right back to the kitchen," said the Greek in red. "I'll consider your punishment later. Quick now, so it won't be too bad. And you, Xikses, had better come out of the pool. If it's a turbot, you're taking a silly chance to stay. I'll have the place drained or screened tomorrow, and we may find what all the pother's been about."

"Then give me a robe," said the one addressed as Xikses. "I lost my tunic somewhere down there."

At this, the guests began laughing again, with an abandon that the excitement and terror of the swift-treading incidents only increased. Posides handed down a robe that someone had discarded and the Mouser, draping it closely about himself, came up. After a moment's joking with some of the others, they moved off.

"Thank you for the diversion," said Posides. "This making fun of Agrippinila is a dangerous business; now it's passed out of their minds."

The Mouser sighed. "Then you knew I was the little turbot-witch."

"Yes, but just because the prank was delightfully childish. When my Roman guests get childish, they get filthy-childish."

The Mouser hooked a beaker of hot wine from a passing slave.

"So Rome's gotten you so that you think it's the mother of vice as well as power?" he said. Posides shook his head.

"No, I don't, but there's no city as nervous as Rome, nor half as anxiety-ridden. And nervousness adds something to plain vice."

"I suppose so; I can see you're a bit more jumpy than I'd ever remembered you. Penalty of wealth?"

Posides changed his mind about wine, and flagged a passing slave.

"Wealth?" he questioned sharply. "It's my poison. I'm never free of business and of hangers-on. Only a freeman, and I have senators' wives a-visiting. No time. Look at it. You've been here over a day, and I've hardly spoken to you."

The Mouser nodded sympathetically, but his eyes looked far away.

"And the emperor's work to fill in your idle moments," he murmured. "Tell me, Posides, isn't he somehow—differently, but somehow—as crazy as Caligula?"

Posides did not look around him.

"Possibly," he said softly after a moment. "The senators would think so if they knew he really wanted to restore the republic. But they insist on considering him diseased, sly, and dangerous. Their nerves are the worst in Rome, and you remember what I just said about Rome. The emperor's the capstone-paradox. A pretty good executive and soldier for a book-worm. I was with him in Britain, too, you know. We Greeks have no cause to complain; he's given us a big push. Only objects to bribes of the nastier sort."

The garden-party showed signs of breaking up; there were gaps now in the buzz of conversation and laughter.

"The reason I wanted to know about him," said the Mouser, "is that he sent me a letter; an offer of employment, apparently."

Posides laughed. "Nothing to fear in that; he has jobs for no end of Greeks. We're his tallyers and counter-tallyers. I'll take you over to the palace tomorrow. Now you must get in and change your clothes. Have you anything on under that cloak I've borrowed?"

"Yes, sewer-mud."

An incredulous smile came into Posides' face. "Then it's really true what that lummox of a slave said about the Greek witch coming up out of the drain?"

"Right. I've been exploring cloaca maxima. I won't burden you with my reasons."

"There are hot baths next to your room. But if you just die of fifteen diseases, you're lucky. You're crazier than you ever were in Cos. Which reminds me: we must talk about the good old island when we get a chance."

"Nothing much has changed there," said the Mouser musingly.

They dodged two drunks, made a side door, turned to look back at a few staggerers in the slightly disheveled garden behind them and the red, sunset-lit city, scrambled but magnificent, beyond the garden walls.

"No," said Posides. "Cos wouldn't change."

He speculatively shook his goblet, saw there was a mouthful of wine left, then raised it. "Xikses," he said through lips that smiled tautly, "I give you a city whose biggest buildings shiver and jump if a dog barks without warning. I give you Rome."

Early next morning, when Xikses came out into the main inner hall, it was to find Posides completing his first spells of business. The Mouser waited in the background, noting that Posides was careful to avoid the appearances of a senator's or of even a citizen's reception. He wore a woolen robe against the morning chill, but it was of a brown stuff, and he encouraged the forms of democratic and casual address even in his humbler petitioners.

"I thank the gods," said an old man with a quavery voice, "that they made me your friend times back. Your help means life for me, come the winter; I am too weak for the bread line and have no son, nor no one to stand for me."

"Bother your tears," said Posides, clapping him on the back, "I owe you much. And whether from me or the line, it is the bread of the kind emperor's getting."

And so breakfast business was at an end and the Mouser came in to Posides, saying, "Nor prosperity, nor luxury, nor vice can teach Rome late rising, O you men of affairs."

"If Rome did not rise, the sun would shirk his climb and stay abed," laughed Posides. "And there's more hurry how; we must be off to Caesar's home, or I am late for work. With luck, you shall see him this week."

"So soon?" queried the Mouser. "And I thought he was an emperor."

"Times are changed," answered the other as an attendant wrapped a light cloak around the Mouser's shoulders. "Come on."

As they followed the narrow street that led from the Esquiline hill towards the Palantine, the number of pedestrians increased, but not greatly. Rome was already at work. The slanting rays of the risen sun promised a hot noonday, and ahead to the left the great marble buildings of the Capitoline and Palantine gleamed milky-gold. That is, when the narrow streets and piled stories of the crowded buildings did not prevent.

"Two men have followed us close for the last three blocks," said the Mouser suddenly and in a low voice.

"My bodyguard," explained Posides. "Necessary because I am close to Caesar; unapparent because I am only a freeman."

The great palace of Caligula, home, too, of the present Caesar, they entered through a garden gate, the way of clerks and secretaries. Posides explained to the guard, who showed him unexpected deference, that his companion was a young Greek whom Caesar desired to employ.

"Every now and then," explained Posides, "the emperor bawls out the guard for taking the ordinary monarchial precautions against assassins. That's why anyone properly accompanied has an easy time."

"You'd almost think that he was trying to bring the republic back," laughed the Mouser. "Think?" said Posides seriously. "Don't be too sure he doesn't mean to do more than think." The Mouser grinned.

"I never thought there had been any republic to bring back. And that, to my way of thinking, means he'll have a better chance of doing it."

A few moments more walking brought them into a large room, evidently once intended for a ridiculously large bedchamber, and therefore now not so inappropriately filled with plain tables, chairs, temporary scroll cases, and a handful of sharp-eyed young Greeks, some little more than boys, busy with wax tables and papyri, with accounts and letters.

For the next three hours, the Mouser sat and watched Posides work as hard as the rest of them.

"We're the emergency tablets," the Greek had explained. "When something comes up that's too much for the treasury, or the Rome secretaries, or the secretaries for provincial matters, or any of the other groups, we have to help. Or matters that can't be classified, or counter-checks on other departments. All that sort of thing."

The Mouser had just about decided to quit drawing vague caricatures on a wax sheet he had picked up, slip quietly out, and do a bit of exploring, when a door—not the one he had entered by—swung open. Doors had been doing that ever since he came in, to permit the passage of the relentless course of business. This was different.

In came a tallish, middle aged man with a limp, thin legs, a pot stomach, a slight stutter, a twitch, and automatic head-tremble, and several other infirmities. He gave the impression of valiantly trying to scurry out from under their weight. At his heels were two soldiers and another of the seemingly endless number of young Greek clerks.

The middle aged man leaned over, laid hold of the foot of a boy-accountant who had dodged under a table, and yanked him out.

"J-j-just because I can't keep soldiers from following me," he said rapidly, "is no reason for any of you thinking there's a sudden execution in the offing. Pluto! But won't anyone ever learn that I'm mild natured? It's never anything but 'The Making of Claudius the Terrible, or A Caligula in Spite of Himself.' There! There! Don't cry. Some day you'll get bigger bribes than anyone ever thought of offering me. Now, gentlemen, all I wanted to know is this: have the offers to the corn-importers been calculated and drawn up?"

"Not quite yet, Caesar," said Posides, "have to finish estimating the losses the government took on the last shipment."

"Dear Jove!" Claudius exploded. "When Romans are starving in a few months, try to feed them stew made out of your loss estimates. Just try! But, better, get on with the offers right now and have them finished by tomorrow if you have to guess the loss estimates. Bribery's so much in your blood that you're more scared than an honest man would be of doing anything without having it all on paper. Now get on with it! Who's that fellow?"

This last remark was accompanied by a head jerk at the Mouser.

"Name is Xikses," said Posides. "He's..."

"Wait, wait," said Claudius, clapping a hand to his forehead. "Let me guess. He's... O, yes...I remember. Heard of him from Xenophon. Wrote him a letter a month ago. And now I like his looks. Come on back with me, Xikses, and I'll tell you what I wanted."

"Wait, Caesar," said the Greek who had come in with the soldiers. "You don't know the man. Search him for weapons, you two."

The soldiers approached the Mouser and patted over his tunic, boot tops, and hair.

"May a thunderbolt hit my tomb," said Claudius, lifting his eyes up. "Doesn't anyone know this is a free country?"

The soldiers completed their search and stepped back.

"Search me, too," said Claudius, lifting up his arms to the soldiers, who only stared straight ahead. "You never think of doing that, do you? And it's so obvious I'm your little pet, aren't I? Could carry twenty daggers, and you'd think no more of them than hairpins. And I knew a girl who was killed with a hairpin. Well, come on, Xikses, I guess they'll let you now. Want to risk it?"

The clerks looked embarrassed, pained, and frightened, but Xikses laughed and stepped forward.

"But, Caesar," said the last appeared Greek, gently and as if to a child, "you unfortunately haven't time for a private conference right now. You'd planned to go down to Ostia to see how the new harbor was getting on."

"Harbor? Visit harbor?" scowled Claudius, and then a grin overspread his face. "Why, Narcissus, that's just the thing. Xikses can come along with me, and then, if I decide to use him, he'll know something of the background. Why, we'll be able to talk about it on the way back and—why—it'll save time. Come alone, all of you, will you? And all of you," (here he suddenly glared at the clerks) "get back to those estimates. An emperors nothing to gawk at, especially me, and you know it. Remember: tomorrow morning!"

For most of the afternoon, the Mouser tagged along after Claudius with Narcissus, feeling very much like a scroll that a busy man has shoved into his cloak—to be read when, and if ever, a chance lull comes into his business. There were other secretaries to visit and a meeting of the college of priests and, sandwiched in between, the reception of a couple of small provincial delegations.

"Dab by dab is the way to do it," Claudius mumbled while mouthing some hastily grabbed hard bread and lettuce. "Official applications—lists and queues—like snakes: knock off the heads each morning and hope that—that way—the tails never get long enough to strangle you."

Later afternoon found them well on the way to Ostia. They had left by the gat that passed just to the left of the granaries, great, silent structures, the mighty community stomachs of the city which made the commercial sounds coming from the emporium behind them distinct but somehow futile-seeming by their very distinctness.

The Ostian Way was comparatively empty. Later, it would be serially dotted by the grain-carts making their daily trip to the city—carried on at late night and early morning to avoid as much counter-traffic as possible. And still later, there would come the return line—often with empty wagons. Rome ate more than it gave.

The Mouser was in the second of the two carriages. With him was Narcissus, who chattered now and again in a fashion that was often as childish as it was witty, but his eyes were bright and darting. Before and behind were a few guards on horseback; their bright armor and accouterment made little clatter. Caesar had set up what proved to be a dicing-board in his carriage, but played solitaire. His companion, a venerable Greek, seemed lost in reverie—though he did not act out by gesture the stages of his reverie, as did the average member of his cultured race.

"Xenophon of Cos, Caesar's physician," Narcissus answered to the Mouser's question. "Never flatters anyone—not even the diseases and let alone the patient. And he isn't even polite enough to gamble."

The Mouser, nodding absently, noticed that the last remark was low enough so that the coachman ahead couldn't have heard it—a habit in making remarks that had been unshakably planted in men during the reign of the late Caligula.

But the Mouser's eyes were fixed ahead on the setting sun, which was lately become strangely dim. On either side of them, the country was rolling and verdant, dotted everywhere with farm horses and truck gardens, and here and there an inn along the way. But the sun, bright all day and now red in its setting, continued to grow dim, and the dazzling, fresh greenness around them became wan, yet more distinct. The sea-fog was coming up ahead of time.

The emperor evidently noticed it, for he left off his idly industrious cup-shaking to wave to the carriage behind and shouted something about hoping "that all the ships were in."

The Mouser saw Xenophon offer him his cloak but omit to help him put it on. And he could imagine a dry remark about every shout being a strain and why not get every bit of rest possible, so why shout?

However, Caesar gave some order to his driver, for his carriage speeded up to a brisk trot and with it the rest of the little cavalcade. The Mouser, even before he came to Rome, had heard a great deal about the work in progress at Ostia to perfect the harbor—the all-essential mouth that received Rome's grain, most of which came from muddy, fertile Egypt. The harbor facilities had been notoriously unsure and even dangerous;

often, the great grain-ships had had to stand off for days, and even weeks, waiting for the calm weather that was essential to even a reasonably safe landing.

Now, the channel was being deepened, mooring and docking space increased, and an artificial island planned to shield the whole. Thousands of workmen were being employed and Claudius was spending on the job the wealth of a dozen minor provinces.

It was natural that he should want to keep in close touch with what was going on, thought the Mouser. That was doubtless why they were speeding up—to beat the twilight, which the fog would greatly shorten.

Before the sun had sunk its breadth again, they were slipping into the port. However, they didn't get by the inevitable delegation, headed by a man who was determined to give a speech that consisted of two scrolls full of thanks to the emperor for booming trade. Claudius fidgeted through the first few lines, and then a happy grin came into his face.

"I sa-ss-ay, and excuse me for interrupting," he said, "But I'm sure that all the streets ahead, down right to the docks, are filled with people. Wonderful patriotism and civic interest, that, and a great compliment to you, their leaders. It's a shame that only a few should hear what you have to say. Now, why don't you get into the carriage behind and give the speech as we ride along?"

The man coughed and said, "Very well, Caesar."

"Everybody gets a dab then," commented Claudius. "And a dab for all's better than no supper at all for most."

"And a bellyache for you and me," whispered Narcissus.

They did not try very hard to help the speechmaker keep his balance as he stood between their legs and got out sentences between jolt-prompted grunts.

The Tale of the Grain Ships

The crowd was mostly composed of workmen returning to the barracks from the scows and the diggings. The streets were as narrow as Rome's, but the air was salt and full of harbor smells, and still they had not come quite to the fog.

They drove rumbling down onto the docks themselves and only paused on the one nearest the sea—a calm sea that lost itself in vapor and that the last light made only the more inky black by contrast.

The terminus of the opposite bank of the Tiber was still visible and the more extensive workings that were there plainly to be seen: new shorings and docks, and a string of barges, two of them equipped with great, mechanical dredges; one could see their superstructures of uprights, beams, pulleys, and ropes looking like dark skeletons.

And now that they were come from out the town onto the docks, a quiet was come down that enabled one to hear the distant talking and singing of the departing workers on the opposite bank. The quiet, indeed, was a little startling. But then, there were only half a dozen ships of any size in the harbor, and they were all riding at anchor, their square sails furled, their oars shipped, and their straight sides high in the water, evidently empty and awaiting cargo.

The speechmaker riding in the second carriage tardily realized that there was no more audience and quit, mumbling, in the middle of a sentence. Narcissus and the Mouser got down, stretched their legs, and slowly made their way forward to where Claudius was listening to the report of the engineer in charge of the operations, one Rufus Licinius.

A couple of slaves started to light torches, but Claudius forbade them, since their glare would make observation impossible. His military escort, now dismounted, therefore stood the closer around him.

"Too slow," broke in Claudius. "We must have more men, barges working from this side, too. And then—but, stay, I haven't heard from you, Encius; I was eager to know if any ships were sighted today. You know, there are four, laden from the granaries of Anciles, two days overdue."

Encius was the harbor-master, a seemingly abstracted man of about forty, with a great black beard.

"Yes, emperor," he replied in a soft voice, "just before the fog came up we glimpsed one, an Egyptian grain-ship from her markings. Doubtless the others are behind—those ships stick close nowadays when they can. She's probably already cast anchor a safe ways out and will be in tomorrow."

"And not even Ostia's present harbor can danger ships in this weather," commented Claudius. "The gods grant that it hold for a month, then a sufficiency at least of this year's crop will be in. She was signaled?"

"When sighted, but the fog came up before we could catch a reply. Those damned Phoenician captains would see to the holystoning of their poop before taking time to reply to a port signal."

"Well, well," muttered Claudius. "A dirty deck induces sea-sickness, so it's—but, now, Rufus, point me out the new location for the shielding island; from what you say the soundings and current observations advise a change. But we want to be very sure before we sink the cement-filled Needle boat. Once down, you know, even the Parthian invasion couldn't raise that."

"True, Caesar," replied Rufus, laughing. "Come here where there's a little better view and I will do my best."

As they moved out to the railing, the soldiers around them and Narcissus and the Mouser behind, they heard two of the soldiers' horses whinny and one rear and plunge, his hooves making a resounding wooden thump as they came down. One of the soldiers swore and went back to quiet them.

"There where I point," Rufus was saying. "And a quarter of a mile out. There's a bar there, and it will make the narrow opening to the north—where it should be."

"Plague the light—I mean the darkness," said Claudius, craning his head forward, a soldier anxiously holding his elbow. "No matter how hard I try, I always get here at the wrong time for looking around. What do you think of it Encius—I mean the new location, not my temporal difficulties?"

"Might be right—better than the old plan, or so it seems to me. With the island further in you'd have to put it further south, and the waves would be higher because of the bar ahead. Still—"

Encius shook his head dubious as if he thought everything connected with the sea hopelessly uncertain, and a good plan worse than a bad one because its inevitable difficulties were apt to prove subtle and bewildering.

"Excellent," laughed Claudius. "This is one of the few times I ever heard you even begin to approve of any plan, Encius. Let me see now: you say that there, Rufus—" and he pointed out in the direction that had previously been indicated.

As the group gazed out with him, the Mouser heard a low throaty noise from Encius, in which surprise and irritation were mingled. It was instantly submerged in a burst of whinnying and cursing and sound of commotion behind them.

He turned to see the horses of the second carriage rear up and the driver, now dismounted, jerked off his feet as he held, either desperately or stupidly, to the bit of one. A kick from the other laid him out and, before attendants could take a hand, both had wheeled and were galloping back off down the dock. There came a crash, as the carriage veered into some crates, but they continued on. The other horses seemed dangerously near to getting out of control, too.

"Holy Livers," stuttered the emperor, excited by the confusion. "What's the matter with them?"

"Can't say, sir," muttered the peering captain of the guard. "They're not new horses, and not new to the sea, either. Hey, there! What happened?"

"We can't tell, sir," shouted the soldier who had first gone back. "Nothing that we could notice scared them. The rest are quieting now, and I'm sending a couple of men back after the ones that bolted."

"Dock attendants will do!"

"Yes, sir."

"Encisus," said Rufus, "What was it that you noticed just before they bolted? I thought—"

"Yes," muttered the port master in a far away voice. "I thought I heard the creaking of oars—just out there..."

As he pointed, the others turned back toward the sea, to feel a breath of damp air brush their faces, and to hear the beginning of a lapping against the piles below their feet. The fog seemed to have come to life and to be moving at a definite pace.

"The grain ship, you mean?" questioned Claudius. Would they try to land—"

"Yes, what could be their reason? Was there anything about the ship when you glimpsed it?" came suddenly from Narcissus.

"We only saw it for a short time," said Encius slowly. "There did seem to be a very bad oar stroke, confused, and only a one-third shift on, if that, but I thought—wait; listen—"

The horses were occasionally quiet now, and, although a wind was coming up, it was from the sea. And with it, it brought distinctly the squeak of oars.

"Yes," whispered Encius. "And now please excuse me, Caesar," he went on, and slowly drew a tremendous breath.

"Ship watchmen, show lights!" he bellowed, so loud and sudden that those around him jumped. "Ship watchmen! Show lights!"

INSANITY

(1)

PRECISELY. BUT SUPPOSE I should go one step farther and tell you that the Inhumans are literally insane?"

After a moment of shocked pause, Jof's mind leaped at the suggestion which had trickled so casually from Regional Director Steel's averted lips. It would explain so much about this balky old world, that refused to go right despite oceans of self-sacrifice and good will. It would clarify a thousand otherwise inexplicable events. A league of ill-intentioned, ill-begotten, brilliant madmen, working without plan or purpose, except to thwart whatever plans for general happiness and lasting peace a dotingly anxious world government tried to put into effect.

It was like seeing, in a tangled skein of gray, a single bright red thread, and realizing that if you pulled out that thread, all the other snarls would automatically fall apart

Then the scientific part of Jof Armandy's mind rebelled. "I wouldn't believe you," he said slowly. "I'd love to go trouble-shooting on that hypothesis. But…madmen can't cooperate. Madmen can't keep secrets. Madmen can't operate efficiently—certainly not with sufficient efficiency to baffle a highly trained, world-wide secret police." A frown creased his black-thatched forehead. "The Inhumans may be evil. In fact, we *know* they're evil. But insane? No."

Regional Director Steel nodded absently. A rueful wisdom gleamed from the half-moons of his averted eyes.

Cultural Advisor McLish nodded too. His sculptured white fingers continued to straighten the objects on his desk. His bushy gray eyebrows twitched in a direction that was a compromise between Steel and the flowing gray mane of which they were the two advance guards.

McLish's nod said, "I told you he'd be sceptical."

The Regional Director studied the side wall, where a window, now opaque, let into the next room. "You repeat the conventional—and politically proper view," he remarked to Jof. "That the Inhumans are a Fifth column of power-hungry, frustrated autocrats. A scum of old-time fascists, communists, capitalists, revolutionists, anarchists, individualists, of Anglo-Americans who can't forget the Wars of the Anglo-American Secession, of Asians who lost out in the Wars of the Asiatic Hegemony, of disgruntled civil service candidates, and of every other species of dissident that these troubled centuries have spawned. In short, the last scrapings of hate—and therefore the most difficult to eradicate—from the history barrel." He rocked on his heels and shoved his hands into the pockets of his drab jacket. "Well, it's understandable that you should take that view. It's the one we've made a point of encouraging, even among our own secret police."

He paused. Jof said nothing. McLish's hands never stopped moving, although they did not ruffle the 21st century silence of the long dark office. His brilliant, pouched eyes were fixed on Jof.

Steel's gaze swung a degree closer.

INSANITY *(1)*

"But how does that conventional view square with the known actions of the Inhumans?" he continued softly, as if arguing with himself. "Does it explain the degree to which the Inhumans often work against their own interests? Does it explain the thousand contradictory rumors they set going? Does it explain why they should blazon their evil intentions to the world, as when they boasted that the secret police could not be disbanded as scheduled, because they constituted too great a threat to world security? Take another concrete example. It's let loose a rumor that the Middle Asian Region was planning to attack the African, and supported it with 'plans of attack' supposedly stolen from Middle Asian headquarters. They might have wanted to stampede the Africans into starting a Civil War. But then why did they then cut the ground from under the feet of the African war party by circulating, a few hours later, forged 'proofs' that the African war party had long been planning an invasion of Middle Asia?" He settled his hands deeper in his pockets. "In short, why do all the actions of the Inhumans add up, on the Maynard Sanity Scale, to a minus-9? And why has every agent that we sent up against the Inhumans reported that he suspected some kind of tie-up with insanity...until he stopped reporting?"

Jof gnawed his lip. The frown stuck. His gaze wandered toward the opaque window in the side wall. "Minus-9, eh? He echoed. "I didn't know anything about that. Or about the agents. So you really think...?"

Steel's gaze swung a degree closer. The half-moons of eyes became gibbous. "A moment ago, Armandy," he murmured, "you said that the Inhumans are evil. But what is evil, if not...?"

Jof shivered faintly—twice. Only the first was a reaction to Steel's implication.

55

FRITZ LEIBER

He had seen a ghost, a murky ghost that swiftly vanished as the wall window went all opaque again, the ghost of a frozen-faced girl with hair blanched like snow in the fashion so popular ten years ago. A power-hungry girl who had dropped a minor trouble-shooter ten years ago, with acid recriminations, because he had refused to take the line of administrative careerism.

What the devil would Harla be doing here? Why she shouldn't want him to see her was easier to understand, considering the circumstances of their parting.

He wondered if the others had noticed. Steel was swung away. McLish played with the objects on his desk, arranging them around a small spool of audiotape.

Suppressing any further reaction, Jof returned to Steel's last remark, which still vibrated potently in his mind despite the interruption.

"But if you know all this about the Inhumans," he said, "why have you kept it a secret?"

"For psychological reasons," replied Steel. "When is a madman most dangerous? When he knows that you think he's crazy. Also, have you considered the effect of such an announcement on the public nerves?"

Jof nodded doubtfully. The murky ghost still peered—in his mind. "Here's an angle," he suggested. "Brainwaves. Those of the insane are unmistakable. With enough receivers, widely distributed, we should be able..."

"Should be," Steel echoed with matter-of-fact irony. "But the Inhumans have invented a shield."

"I see. And all the secret agents you've sent out thus far have been—"

"Or come back insane themselves. Hopelessly, unreachably insane." Steel's voice was not a whisper, quite. "It is only five days since the last one, Will Manders—you knew him, didn't you—was committed to Mindcrest Sanitarium. The madmen we are up against seem to understand the method of madness."

"Very well," said Jof, straightening up a bit. "And you want me to—"

"It's a glorious opportunity," McLish cut in, anticipating Jof's answer. He seemed to have been waiting for this moment. His mellow voice boomed dramatically. One didn't need to be told that the Cultural Advisor had been a renowned literary and verbal artist before answering the call of the higher art of politics. "Only think—for fifty years now only one thing has stood between man and the perfect freedom that is his due. Only one great ugly secret thing—the threat of the Inhumans. To eliminate that threat, to number yourself as one of that small band who have gone out unaided and alone, to be perhaps the one who—"

"Yes, of course I'll go." Jof stood up. "Am I to be furnished with any further information?"

McLish pushed the audiotape toward him, down an avenue fence by the other small objects.

He said, "You have approximately one half hour in which to commit the contents to memory. Then the impressions will automatically disappear."

Jof picked up the spool. "One last angle," he said. "What psychiatrists are in on this? How about conferring with someone like Dr. Maynard out at Mindcrest? Guardedly, if necessary."

Facing away, Steel shook his head. "It is not advisable," he said. "The tape will explain."

Jof nodded, but in his mind was the germ of a plan, or at least of an intention.

The faint whish of the door contracting behind him sliced a shaving off the silence, left it as solid as before. McLish leaned back, exhaled, glanced enviously at Steel.

"He believes everything you told him," he remarked. "You handled him with exquisite subtlety."

Steel did not move.

McLish concealed his disappointment under a cloak of elaborate verbiage. "We are the most fortunate of rulers," he mused. "Scapegoats are a necessity for any healthy society. The equation of government can only be balanced by the cancellation—liquidation—of certain factors—political opponents. And that in turn requires the addition of one more factor—the scapegoat. But former governments have had to employ real scapegoats, which was inconvenient, because real scapegoats are apt to rebel or act as focuses of sympathy and discontent. Whereas we—"

"Armandy's being followed?" Steel broke in sharply, still motionless.

"Of course. A woman. One who I am sure will find the task of checking up on him highly distasteful—but stimulating." He chuckled. "You know, Steel, I have only the most abject admiration for the consistency with which you keep up this pretense. This admirable illusion. This perfect absorber of blame. This scapegoat that can never strike back..."

Steel turned a little. He seemed to look at McLish crookedly, as if the whites of his eyes could see.

"The Inhumans really exist," he said.

McLish's jaw dropped. It worked a little, but no word came out. Every flicker of brilliance departed from the pouched eyes. There was never a more perfect picture of complete dumbfoundment.

"And they are really insane," Steel finished.

INSANITY (1)

JOF TURNED THE controls of his jetabout over to the phlegmatic gate-attendant and entered Mindcrest Sanatarium in the prescribed way—by walking.

In a minute the wind-freighted pines had closed around him, sending down infrequent cool dribbles of the recent rain. The glimmer of the gate quickly faded. The pathlight was just sufficient to show roots and turns—not enough even to register as artificial.

One quickly sensed the wisdom of Dr. Maynard's prescription. Here in the dark, away from the rush of scooters, the flash of signal lights, the tingle of power transmission beams, the maze of regulations, and the consciousness of government spies, himself included, it might have been the Twentieth Century—B.C. as well as A.D. Soothing giant hands seemed to lift the weight of the world away and stroke the jangled nerves.

Jof gratefully snuffed the damp, resinous air and enjoyed the feel of the gravel, faithfully transmitted in diminished form through his shoes' thick, sensitive soles. He hadn't realized until now how much the last hours had taken out of him, how great a strain it was to know *the secret*—to look for the signs of warped thoughts in each passing face, to listen to the chatter of commentators and the hum of small talk with the feeling that any moment it might rise to the cackle of hysterical laughter, to sense the vast irrational ocean of unconscious thought, on which sanity was only a frail ship beating through the storm.

He chuckled. Already it seemed long ago that he had scanned the gate-tender's glum, weathered face suspiciously!

There was a shuffling in the leaves—some night animal.

Perhaps he was settling down to his new job. At any rate, he'd take advantage of the respite afforded by the woods. Resolutely he kept his thoughts off the job ahead, even when the lights of Mindcrest began to glow mysteriously between the pine boles.

The shuffling was repeated. Jof stopped. It came again— louder, nearer, too clumsy for any four-footed animal.

Jof's nerves were tight again.

The shuffling stopped.

After a pause the voice came, whiningly, as if it were a fragment of the wind.

"Hello, Jof Armandy. Out looking for the same thing I got, aren't you?"

Jof told himself there was no justification for the gust of panic that went through him when he recognized the voice. After all, he knew that Will Manders was here, and what sort of place this was.

But his eyes still strained at the darkness, though he managed to keep his voice casual as he replied, "Hello, Will. I was hoping to meet you. But how did you know I was coming?"

The wind laughed. "I heard your thoughts, Jof. They cut something out of my brain so I could hear their thoughts and be controlled. But sometimes I hear things I'm not supposed to."

Paranoia, Jof told himself as he took a shivering step toward the voice. Delusions of persecution. Both Steel and the wire averred that Manders had been committed to Mindcrest five days ago, hopelessly insane.

Driven insane by the Inhumans.

But that still left the problem of how they had managed to drive him insane.

"That's right, Jof. They did it by cutting something out of my brain. I'm not paranoid, though they can make me have paranoid delusions whenever they want to—suspicions of Steel and the World Government and the whole world, as if everything were leagued against me. You see, I *can* hear your thoughts, though there's a crazy buzzing that almost blankets them, for your mind hasn't had the thing cut out of it yet. You don't yet know what it is to have insanity streaming at you from a dozen minds stronger than your own."

The gravel rutched under Jof's feet. His cold, sweaty hands touched a tree trunk. "But if they can control you," he challenged the darkness, "how is it that you can tell me about it?"

"Sometimes they aren't watchful. And they didn't think I'd be able to hear anyone's thoughts but theirs. I heard your thoughts coming through the ceaseless massed buzz of the world's minds, like the hum of a billion machines. I heard your thoughts climbing up the plateau toward Mindcrest. There came a break in their control. I slipped out to meet you."

Jof stopped groping. His hands dropped to his sides.

"What can I do, Will?" he asked.

"For me, nothing. I'm theirs. They'll have me back soon."

"Not for keeps. Who are they, Will? How can we get at them?"

The reply was halfway between a whimper and mockery. "I don't know, Jof. I don't know. They've caught me and taken something out of my brain and made me their slave, and still I don't know who they are or where they are, except that when I look in snatches through the eyes of one of them I see a wall with a blue star, and except that I think some of them may be here in Mind…"

Without warning the voice rose in a shattering scream to a peak that seemed to consist of the word "No" twice repeated, and broke off in cackling laughter.

Bright light drenched the place. Beyond the tree was Manders, still standing but strangely slumped, like a scarecrow.

The light bobbed closer, reached Mander's side. The man immediately behind it said, "Hello, old chap. You'd better get back to the house. Mart will go with you." A big capable arm went around Mander's shoulder, facing him up the gravel path, guiding his listless footsteps.

The man behind the light stayed. He directed it against the gravel, so that his face became visible too. He was tall and thickchested with a broad, white, small-featured face. He looked at Jof with mild curiosity.

Jof became conscious of the beads of sweat trickling down his forehead.

"My name's Armandy," he said, and explained about his arrangements for a meeting with Dr. Maynard.

The big man nodded. "Of course." And they started up the hill.

But the mysterious lights of Mindcrest were no longer to Jof the symbols of a soothing escape from dangerous realities. Instead, he was thinking what an apt place of concealment a madhouse would be for madmen with a method. The feel of the inner belt of specialized equipment around his waist was reassuring.

"That chap who had the seizure," said Sline, nodding ahead. "You happen to know him?"

"I'd met him before," Jof replied cautiously. "It was quite a shock."

"A very puzzling case. His case-history isn't apparently the usual paranoids."

"He's confined?"

"Not at all." Sline's eyes probed sideways. "There's practically no confinement at Mindcrest."

INSANITY (7)

They went on a few steps. "It's rather lonely work up here, I'd imagine," Jof remarked.

"Oh no. Mindcrest's a world in itself—a world set apart. And then there's the privilege of working under Maynard."

They had passed through a modest door and into a green, spongy-floored corridor, before the pines had thinned enough to give Jof much of a view of the place.

"Mindcrest's like that—a lot bigger than you realize," Sline observed. "And with more ramifications. Our pioneer work in space psychoses puts us in touch, in a way, with the whole outside cosmos. That's my specialty—" and he was embarked on a discussion of the strange mental obstacles that hindered the work of those who ventured outside the stratosphere.

Jof half listened to descriptions of cosmic shock and gravitational dementia, and of the pseudo-gravitational devices used in treating the latter, while the active part of his mind was engaging in appraising the value of the information he had gotten from Will Manders.

"Of course," Sline remarked, "space exploration isn't so much thought of these days, what with the other planets turning out so inhabitable and, at first glance, uninteresting. Rather like Antarctica in the Twentieth Century. But it will be, some day. I was a spaceman myself, you know," he said casually, tapping his forehead, "until some kink up here stopped me. Now I take it out in studying the kinks. Right ahead is our amphi-planetarium where we do some of our most important work. Perhaps you'd care to see it?"

OPAQUE CORRIDOR

THE PATIENTS IN this section," explained Dr. Frobisher quietly, "are all spacemen, and all of them suffer from some morbid fear of space. Some of them are in various stages of cosmic shock, which is analogous to wartime shell-shock, as you probably know. A few have a touch of gravitational dementia. They refuse to recognize gravity. They would throw themselves down from heights if they got the chance, thinking they could not fall. Others, of course, have suffered physically as well as mentally and have to be hospitalized regularly for recurrent Venusian fever, cosmic ray burns, or the like. Each case has its own peculiarities."

"I see no windows or transparencies," observed the visitor in that hushed and reverent voice laymen usually adopted.

"There are none. As I told you, these patients are all alike in having a morbid fear of space. Sight of the sky, especially the night sky with its stars, would send them into convulsions superficially similar to those of epilepsy or insulin shock. They are earth-bound in a very literal sense. Of course psychiatry has always recognized agoraphobia—fear of being in the open. But these spacemen manifest it in an exaggerated and novel form. Especially involved is their sense of vision. It is the sight of the heavens they cannot stand. Hence the artificial illumination and the absence of windows. This section of Morningview Sanatorium is known as 'opaque corridor.'"

"Their chance of recovery?" whispered the visitor.

"Fifty-fifty, or perhaps a little less. Sometimes the cure is gradual. Occasionally, though rarely, it comes as the result of what you might call a self-imposed shock. Two weeks ago one of the gravitational dementia patients escaped and threw himself down from the third storey. Suffered severe internal injuries as well as compound fractures of the left leg and arm. An attempt to remove his liver for treatment outside the body failed. But before death supervened his mental condition was much improved—much improved."

The visitor repressed a shiver at this cold-blooded enthusiasm.

"However," Doctor Frobisher hastened to add, "fully a third of the cases get progressively worse and become complicated by paranoia, with its delusions of persecution, or some other primitive insanity."

"Poor fellows," murmured the visitor dutifully. "To think that these men were once pioneering Mars and Venus, or manning the rocketships that serve the mines on the moon. Some of the faces look familiar. That big chap over there especially, the one with his head bent down at an unnatural angle."

"Naturally you recognize him. That's Sven Christofferson, one of the survivors of the second trans-Mars exploratory unit. The bent-neck posture is rather common. Result of a morbid fear of looking up."

"Poor fellow," repeated the visitor inadequately. "Even now he looks like a Viking. The sort of man you'd trust to pilot a rocket ship anywhere. Such strong features, competent hands. Yes, I remember reading about him several times. To think he has a half billion miles of spacing to his credit. And now this!"

"An interesting case," agreed the doctor briskly. "An almost perfect textbook example of space-fear, uncomplicated by any other symptoms. Christofferson has been with us for eleven months. At present his mental condition is approaching a crisis. Either he will begin to respond to treatment or else— and it's more likely—true insanity in the form of paranoia will supervene."

"He looks calm enough," said the visitor. There was an uncomfortable pause. Then he frowned and added the remark the doctor had heard a hundred times: "I wonder just what he's thinking about?"

For the past two months things had been getting progressively worse with Sven Christofferson. The easy periods, when he understood things, were getting fewer and fewer, and the black periods were getting longer and less bearable. Just now he felt that the ceiling was getting thinner and thinner, until presently holes would burst open in it and the *fear* would spurt through at him and the stars would find out where he was hiding and come after him. Oh, he still knew that that was nonsense, all right, but the temptation to hug the floor and crawl under a table was getting damnably irresistible. He must fight it. God knows, the bent neck was bad enough.

Not to be able to look up. Not to be able to stand the sight of the stars and the black heavens, the space that had once been a challenge to him. Why, it was the most pitiful and childish affliction that man could experience. It was like a return to prehistoric ages, when men crept into caves and cowered from the comet and the eclipse. Opaque corridor! Better anything than this disheartening and infinitely exasperating torture. Yet if he saw so much as a patch of sky he knew he would writhe and twist and blubber like an idiot.

And what was the eventual fate in store for him? Insanity. Christofferson knew only too well. Only yesterday hadn't he broken down and screamed and run amuck, swearing that Venusian worms were crawling in after him through the water pipes? He had refused to drink water or let attendants bathe him. They had had to put him in a wet pack. And one of these days he would go the same way as Andrews. His mind would snap for once and all. Anything would be better than that. Anything. Even suicide.

Suicide. The idea took hold of him as strongly as if he'd been thinking about it unconsciously for months. And no sooner did the idea enter his head than the fear of true insanity began to drive him toward an irrevocable decision.

To conceal his excitement from the watchful attendants, he made a pretense of looking around him casually. Clad in pyjamas and slippers, he was sitting in the central lounging room of opaque corridor. Behind the transparency in the west wall he noticed Doctor Frobisher talking to a stranger. Sitting across from Sven in one of the comfortable sponge-synthetic arm chairs was Rev Williams. Rev Williams was another spaceman whose mind had been driven over the edge by fear. At one time he had been the highest ranking naviga-tor on the Earth-Moon geode. Now he was tearing paper into various peculiar shapes. He lived in mortal terror of the stars, and anything associated with the stars. Once he had fright-ened himself into a fit by tearing out a piece of paper that was star shaped.

The sight of Williams fixed Sven Christofferson's deter-mination. He felt curiously aloof, like a psychiatrist inspecting the end product of space-fear, and at the same time horribly shaken and terrified. Yes, suicide! That was the half-sane man's escape from insanity. If only he had died on his last trip out. If only the second trans-Mars exploratory unit had never returned. That was the right sort of death for a spaceman. But now he could neither live nor die like a spaceman.

Doctor Frobisher had entered the lounging room. Sven shrunk from the scrutiny of the coldly penetrating eyes, hugging to himself his guilty determination. But he knew that Frobisher would notice any change in his manner and make deductions therefrom, so he attempted to make his manner as casual as possible.

"How are things with you, Sven?" said the doctor in a brief, matter-of-fact voice.

Sven shrugged his shoulders.

"Feeling no different, eh?"

Sven nodded. The doctor eyed him sharply for a moment, then walked on. In front of a door in the east wall he hesitated for a moment, as if an idea had come to him. Then he extracted a slim key from his pocket, unlocked the door and slipped through it, carefully drawing it shut behind him. Sven knew that the door led to a small vestibule that opened onto the roof of the east wing. The thought of the flat, open space made him sick. It was evening now, he remembered, though there was no difference in the appearance of opaque corridor, and the stars were out, the bright horrible stars.

What if he were to go truly insane before he managed to kill himself? The thought terrified him, goaded him on like a lash. He must kill himself before the fear overwhelmed him, before the holes opened in the thinning roof and the stars found him out. But how? Here in opaque, surveillance was almost constant. There were no sharp edges, no cords. All that had been taken into consideration. If only he could escape to the roof which was four stories high—but that was utterly impossible, ironically! His fear held him trapped between these walls. He could no more walk out onto that roof than fly.

Suddenly Sven dug his fingers into the yielding sponge-synthetic. No, by heavens, there was perhaps a way! If he managed to get access to the roof, and if he *blindfolded* himself. Then, with his fear of paranoia driving him on, he might be able to force himself to the edge. Once at the edge, nothing could stop him from taking the plunge. In a second it would all be over. Could he do it, though? Desperately he thrust all such questions from his mind. He must make the attempt. He *must* die. The fear of paranoia would be enough to balance the fear of space, until it was all over.

But how get on the roof? Frobisher would be coming back that way shortly. But he would be sure to relock the door. Unless...unless some sudden emergency distracted him. Sven's eyes sought out Rev Williams. Instantly Sven saw how he would be able to create such an emergency. It was a cruel way, but it might work. He took a piece of paper and began carefully to tear it according to a certain pattern. The pattern of a star. Then he waited for Frobisher to return.

Had his mind already snapped, he wondered, that he should think such a crazy plan had any chance of success? But no, he mustn't stop now. He must go through with it. He would *make* it succeed. As if he were a man condemned to certain death, thoughts of his past life came back to plague and distract him. The thrill of his first flight from earth as a student spaceman. The jolt of the atomic-drive rockets. The momentary, breathtaking pull of inertia. The feel against his skin of the tight, thick space-jacket, which he had always vaguely associated with something he had read about the chain armor of a medieval knight. Those had been days without fear, days when a man didn't give more than a second thought to the veterans who were ray-burnt or space-drunk or cosmic-shocked from too much spacing. He recalled how he had been impressed by seeing the sun dwindle when he was on a ship that was rocketing for Mars, how he had felt dwarfed by the gigantic sun that beat down on the steaming Venusian jungle. Homesickness had meant little then, just an occasional emotional tug toward the shining planet that was Earth. But then, on that trans-Mars expedition, the expedition he'd been so proud to sign on, it had suddenly grown to overwhelming proportions. Within six days it had turned him into a slobbering wreck, whose every tortured nerve cried out for the solidity of Earth. A miserable agoraphobia who tried to hide himself in the caves and tunnels of a disordered imagination, who sometimes had cried like a baby because he knew that Morningview Sanatorium was built *above* ground. Morningview! The very name was ironic. Why was man cursed with nervous and emotional systems insufficiently stable to stand up under the strains his ambition imposed upon them? All life was a gigantic irony.

The door in the east wall was opening slowly. Biting his under lip, Sven slid the paper star along the floor with his foot to where Williams could see it. The effect was almost instantaneous. Williams made a noise that was half grunt and half scream. Then he leaped to his feet. Halfway across the room he sprawled on the floor, twisting in convulsions. Doctor Frobisher hurried over toward him, leaving the door open behind him. In an instant Sven was through it and in the vestibule. Covering his eyes with his left hand, he pushed open the door to the roof.

The impact of the openness was something that struck him like a physical blow. It forced him to his knees. He felt as if the rays of the stars were boring like silver gimlets into his brain. At first he felt utterly powerless to move further. All his instincts cried out for the confinement of opaque corridor. And he felt a crazy, perverse temptation to uncover his eyes. If he did that, he knew he would be lost.

The struggle only lasted a few seconds. The fear of para-noia proved strongest. Slowly he crawled across the rough sur-face of the roof, unconscious of his trembling and the cold sweat that poured down his forehead. Finally his hand struck the outer railing. Laboriously, he pulled himself upright.

It was then that the temptation to look at the sky returned. He did not fight it. He felt like a man already dead. One look, he thought, one last defiance to the stars that had broken his life. Then the final plunge. Nothing could stop him now.

He raised his head, drew back his left hand, and opened his eyes. A needle of light pierced his eyes. It was Rigel, green Rigel in Orion. The star they had aimed at in the trans-Mars expedition. And there was yellow Betelguese, the giant. He pulled himself up a little on the railing, then paused. It was a clear night, no moon, the sky between the stars deep blue like ink. His eyes sought out red Aldebaran and glittering Sirius.

Suddenly he began to wonder where he was and what he was doing. He was supposed to be afraid, wasn't he? And this sleek, metal railing, he was supposed to throw himself down from it, wasn't he? But why? He wasn't afraid at all. Vaguely he remembered how he'd been living in a place without windows, and how he had just done a cruel thing to a man named Rev Williams. Frightened him with a paper star and sent him into a fit. Yes, that was it. This place was an asylum. Morningview. He had been here for months. But he wasn't afraid.

Gradually his grip eased on the railing, and he turned around. A little gray-haired man with cold, penetrating eyes was standing there. Behind the little man were two muscular-looking fellows dressed in white. He ought to know the man. Wasn't he…yes, he was called Frobisher!

And with that his memory came swiftly back. He looked at Doctor Frobisher carefully, as if he were searching his face for some clue.

Finally Sven said, "You knew then? I mean you knew that I was going to attempt suicide, and you let me go ahead with it?"

The doctor nodded.

"But why? Why? Did you think it might…help me?"

Again the doctor nodded.

"Yes, I did think just that," he said in his quick, clipped way. "I could tell that your case was reaching a peculiar sort of climax. Half an hour ago I read the idea of suicide in your face as clearly as if it had been printed there. Of course, I saw through your ruse to get out onto the roof. I took the chance."

"How about Williams?" asked Sven with sudden anxiousness. "Have I hurt him badly?"

The doctor shook his head.

"Very little," he said, and then added briskly, "It's rather cold out here. Although you may have forgotten, it's almost winter. You'd better come back inside now. Not to opaque corridor, but to the section for convalescents and those under observation."

Sven felt dizzy and a little strange in the head, as though a thousand hands had just been reaching around inside his skull, rearranging things.

But he lifted up his head again and shook his fist at the vault of the heavens. He cried at the stars in a thin voice that had the ghost of a laugh.

"Just wait a little and I'll be coming up there after you."

PREDATOR UNIVERSE

I.

MARTIN KRUGER WAS nervous, but it wasn't his usual sort of nervousness, and that alone made it almost exhilarating. His usual sort of nervousness was a dead, but still writhing state of mind, in which cigarette smoke became corrosive, his typewriter a dusty instrument of torque, the books lining the walls of Mammoth Encyclopedias' editorial office a prison wall threatening momently to close even the windows and doors, and the clock on the wall a measure of eternity. This nervousness, on the other hand, was very much alive.

A sudden burst of typing made him look quickly over his shoulder. Paunchy old Tregarron was jabbing at his machine maliciously, as if he were doing sly dirt to someone—possibly the archangels, since that must be the article he was engaged on, though he usually chose victims whose winces could be seen or at least more easily visualized. Perhaps he had found a way to introduce an anti-labor slant into his article on the police captains of Heaven. His thick jowl was flattened against his dirty shirt as he typed along concentratedly. Tregarron always did have that look of an arena spectator waiting. Why was it that the church attracted such hypocritical, lewd people these days? Though if you could believe the story going around, even the church had cast out Tregarron. And why should he raise the question at all, since he was uncertain in his mind whether the church deserved better men?

As he turned back, with an incongruous avoidance of making the slightest noise, more like a man in a jungle than a man in an office, he noticed that Sam Bernstein was watching him. Martin wondered if his nervousness was that obvious. He shouldn't have told Sam about his childhood. Ever since then, Sam had been waiting for him to go into a fit or a trance.

Dumpy Mrs. Crothers marched over to the wall and, standing on tiptoes, finally managed to ease down the big atlas. She made a slight "Hhmf!" sound to rebuke Sam and the new chap for not offering to help, though the latter probably would have if she'd just given him a look. Then she pulled down her skirt where it had hiked up, and came marching back.

It was really a very dull afternoon, thought Martin, the sort that made everyone long for the three o'clock break, when they went down for cokes.

And yet he was nervous. There was something astir in the office, or in the droning city around it, or even beyond that. The one small patch of sky visible to him seemed too dark a blue. He almost expected to see a star in it, as if he were at the bottom of a well. It was like the trajectory of a gun being trained on him from infinity.

Another flurry of sound made him look involuntarily behind him. This time it was Sam abruptly starting an argument with the new chap about what was going to happen to the world in the next few years. In short order Sam had it atom-bombed to bits and was gloomily disdaining to pick up the pieces, and the new chap was "if"ing and "but"ing with the same uncertainty he had shown this morning when he had been given a stack of ancient articles pasted on sheets of cardboard and told he was to modernize them with the aid of two other encyclopedias, an unabridged dictionary, and a child's book of knowledge.

The new chap hadn't learned yet that people didn't argue at Mammoth to arrive at conclusions, but only to express a mood, though he was probably beginning to get a glimmering that his job was to help make superficially presentable a set of books that would be sold at startlingly low, but nevertheless profitable prices to people who clipped coupons from newspapers or attended movie houses on "book night."

As Sam launched into a description of the socialist organization which alone could save the world from destruction, but which regrettably was quite impossible of achievement, Martin felt a faint twinge of guilt, hardly distinguishable from boredom, and began touching up with a blue pencil the more clumsy expressions in Mrs. Crothers' article on Antarctica. A phrase, "earth's coldest, loftiest, and most desolate continent," occurred to him. Without stopping to analyze the reason for its disproportionate satisfyingness, he inserted it at the beginning.

He started as Mr. Peters dumped a sheaf of proof on his desk, though Mr. Peters was the mildest and most affable of men, as well as the tiniest. After the inevitable consultation on the two or three choice questions of grammar and style Mr. Peters had thoughtfully saved for him, the proof-reader crinkled his little mustache with a solicitous smile and remarked, "By George, you don't look quite as chipper as usual, if I may say so. I trust you're not getting a cold."

Martin disclaimed the possibility and sent Mr. Peters away beaming with happiness at the well-being of his fellow men, but then he began to wonder. There couldn't be anything wrong with him physically; it wasn't two weeks since he'd had that check-up at the clinic. But then why this nervousness, this mounting jumpiness, with a silly but undeniable tinge of premonition to it, as if, to use a fanciful parallel, he alone of all men in the city knew that the atom-bomb, to which Sam had stridently returned, even now, was due to hit in a very few minutes.

Sam's voice continued to rise, and from the desk facing Martin's, Tom Donnelly looked up frowningly—something that Tregarron and Mrs. Crothers had been waiting for him to do for the past ten minutes. The new chap embarrassedly tried to get back to his article on alchemy, but Sam only talked the louder. After a moment Tom returned to the sheets that Martin knew were the outline of his new detective story. Being the chief editor at Mammoth, Tom Donnelly did more outside work during office hours than anyone else.

Beyond Tom's desk, Tea Janecek stopped typing and began to rummage around for her cigarettes. Martin watched her uneasily, a tall, pale-armed girl with horn-rimmed glasses and a kindred stylishly armored attractiveness. Finally she stood up to see better and found the package behind her typewriter. As she leaned over, Martin saw a little more of her desirable breasts than the square-cut neck of her black dress ordinarily revealed. He winced.

The telephone on his desk jangled. It was Marion.

"Hello, dear."

"Oh, hello," he murmured, a bit flusteredly.

"Are you all right?"

"Sure."

"I just felt like calling you up."

"Sure, darling."

"Oh, and there is one thing, I wish you'd pick up some liquor on your way home. Professor Ainsworth happened to phone and I invited him for dinner."

After a pause, she asked, "You're not mad, are you?"

"No, no, not at all," he assured her, hurriedly recalling his mind from the thirty-hear backward plunge it had taken. Why should he be disturbed by Ainsworth just because Ainsworth had known him when he had been a freakish child prodigy, a fascinating problem for the university psychologists, possessed or rather supposedly possessed of supernormal sensory ability, a subject for telepathy and clairvoyance experiments. What difference did that make?

"It's been months since we've seen him," he continued. "How is the old coot, anyway."

"His old self, so far as I could tell. You know, sort of ghostly and benign."

Martin chuckled. "A rather gutsy ghost. Did he seem to have anything special on his mind?"

"Not that he mentioned. He said he was calling from the science building."

"Uh huh," commented Martin, faintly wondering what the old student of mind could have been doing in the temple of matter.

"Oh, and we had a bit of excitement this morning just after you'd gone," Marion continued.

"Just a minute, Dear," Martin interrupted, as Mrs. Crothers laid some articles on his desk, ostentatiously avoiding looking at the blue-penciled Antarctica sheets.

"Here are Albania, Albany, and Andorra," she informed him. "I didn't notice you were telephoning."

"Thanks, thanks a lot, I'll look at them right away," he told her as she about-faced. Then he said to Marion, "Okay."

"It really isn't anything. I don't want to bother you if you're busy."

"No, go ahead."

"Well, about a half hour after you left I happened to look out the front window and I noticed two men with little black boxes. I thought they were from the water department, though that didn't seem quite right. When they'd gone down the street, Mrs. O'Brien came running over wiping her hands on a dish-towel and assured me they were men from the university 'testing for atoms.' And then she repeated those scare stories about the uranium pile being responsible for cases of sterility. 'Four in this block that I know for certain, Mrs. Kruger,' she said, and then she sort of took me in and added, 'and maybe five.'"

Martin chuckled. "The old fool."

"Well, I'm not entirely sure—" Marion broke off. "Anyway, I told her I was sure the radioactivity couldn't have done anything, but she just went on about sterility and cancer, with all sorts of juicy death bed details, and when she left she stopped outside the door and looked toward the university and put her hand on her bosom and said, 'Mind me well, Mrs. Kruger, those atoms aren't going to bring any good to people. They shouldn't have stirred them up.' Well, I didn't mean to talk your ear off."

"It was fun."

"You're all right?"

"Of course."

"Good-bye, dear."

"Bye."

Martin put down the phone. He wondered if Marion could have noticed his nervousness, decided against it. "Are you all right?" was just a stock phrase, the words of modern love, a kind of universal greeting in this worried age. Why wonder at nervousness? Everyone was nervous, the futile nervousness of confined animals overwhelmed by technology, whipped on by advertising, constantly urged to think and act, only to find that at every point people with a keener eye for profit had done the thinking and acting for them, goalless, soulless, connected by only a few overworked nerve fibers with the phantom world of film, newsprint, radio voices, and other standardized delights, entirely severed from any larger, richer reality, if there was one.

This office was a parable of it, a pantomime. Tregarron was Religion, a fat, earth-bound deity savouring the fumes of those singed by the times. Mrs. Crothers was Geography, clutching Asia in one stubby hand, while the necklace of the Antilles dripped from the other. Sam Bernstein was Literature—the full-throated voice shrunk to a querulous murmur. Tea Janecek was Art, as skeletal and contrived as a surrealist picture done to grace a snobbish show-window. The new chap was Science, or would be, if he showed the necessary mediocrity. History, Government and Biography were farmed out to three equally meager-spirited hacks. While he, Martin, God or God's inexistence help him, was, along with his supervisory work, a chain-smoking, empty-headed Philosophy!

In the excitement of the picture he jerked to his feet and paced away from his desk. Sam Bernstein started to get up, then glanced at the clock, apparently deciding that it wasn't quite time yet for cokes, resumed his needling of the new chap. Martin swerved past Mrs. Grother's desk and stood by the window, kneading his palms with his fingers, curling his toes in his shoes. To his surprise, his little sardonic outburst of imagination hadn't got rid of his nervousness, but rather heightened it—or at least somehow it had become heightened. One thing he was sure of, though: whatever his nervousness' source, it wasn't in the room behind him—those six pillars of wisdom were a part of the walled-in, impotent world where he too was confined. His nervousness came from beyond.

There was a touch of apprehension in it, but he liked the vividness it imparted to things. That immense gray facade across the way, pierced with typist-peopled windows, the blank brick walls beyond that, the sooty signs, the grotesque chimneys and ventilators and black water-tanks, like bric-a-brac atop the mantlepieces of giants, the ornate steel filigree of the elevated station, the distant towers topped by beacons or flags or faceless statues—all that absurd and menacing geometry was tangible. And beyond that the sun-pelted sky, churning with winds, adrift with clouds, buffeted by the wings, propellers, perhaps roaring jets. And beyond even that, unseen but terrifically real, the dusty, meteor-riddled void, the plunging planets, the greater void, the other suns and worlds, the still greater void, the other islands of stars, the utmost rim of space—and perhaps beyond even that, other cosmoses, other blind pockets of existence.

Suddenly he was afraid. All that out there, that seemed so rock-ribbed in daily life, was really so insubstantial. How could we be sure of it from one moment to the next? How could we have the faintest inkling of what it intended? Science had weighed and measured, men had lived and died, but that proved nothing, and a million years of the past in no way guaranteed one second of the future.

The feeling grew in his mind of something cold and inscrutable watching him from the depths of space, something that saw clean through him, something that intended to play with him as a cat with a mouse. For a moment it became so strong that he ducked back out of view—and immediately started to snicker at his silliness. But then he turned and grew silent, for the room had changed.

Oh, it was the same room, all right, and superficially everything was as it should be. Tom Donnelly was scribbling a correction in his outline, Mrs. Crothers was hunting a name on a map, Sam was puffing words and smoke, the new chap was nodding as he reached for a dictionary, Tea Janecek was shaving the ash of her cigarette, Tregarron was stealing a glance at her over his glasses. But they were all too real, too vivid, bathed in some equivalent of that brassy glow that sometimes comes after the sun has set. Details stood out like master touches in a picture—Mrs. Crother's white finger inching wormlike across Africa, the tiny black arabesque flowing from Tom's soft pencil, the glint on Tregarron's glasses, all of them unbearably highlighted. And there swept over Martin the realization that this sort of thing had happened to him before, and simultaneously the memory of when and where it had happened—blindfolded on a chair, jabbered at by psychologists, asked to achieve the impossible—and now, as then, he didn't know what was going to happen, and he was very frightened.

He managed to get back to his desk, he started to sit down, and then—

The universe vanished.

The next thing he knew he was lying on his back on the floor.

SOCIAL INVENTOR

ANY INVENTOR HAS a tough time bucking public opinion, but the social inventor has it toughest of all. Invent the safety pin or the transistor and you at least have a shiny gadget to show around. But invent the semi-brother or the multifamily or a scheme for pain free divorce that practically eliminates it, and people are shrugging their shoulders and hollering "Foul!" at the same time.

Fact is that folks have an extraordinary blindness for and at the same time a deep suspicion of social gadgets. They don't class them as inventions at all. Of course they sometimes give a few squeaky cheers when a big nation adopts representative democracy, but who ever clapped the inventor? Everyone knows about Thomas Edison and even Luther Burbank but who remembers John Humphrey Noyes, pioneer of positive eugenics and a primitive form of the multifamily? And people are already beginning to forget Jimmy Villon, inventor of the above-mentioned gadgets and a slew of others, although if anybody has done more to put elbow room into the Age of Conformity, and cure the atom-bomb itch, yes and even begin to bridge the gulf between customer-directed and commissar-directed cultures, I'd like to know!

No sage looked in on Jimmy age seven and said, "Mark me, this child will change the world." The only tributes to his early inventiveness were a father and mother who quit quarreling and a younger brother and sister who take care of each other instead of being a drag on the young genius who had been sent to take care of them—and any suggestion that these were clear applications of the reverse mutual-friction formula and the infanticosm would have been considered a one-way ticket to the loony bin.

By the time Jimmy got invited to college because of several simple pedogogical gadgets he created strictly from hunger for knowledge, a few people around him sensed that he was up to something, but they weren't sure what. A social inventor is always getting a "Dreadful Motives" sign pinned to the back of his coat while he isn't looking! Either he's power-mad, or a world-saver, or a dilettante, a thwarted headshrinker, a brand-bearing witchburner or booze-bearing bohemian, an uninstitutionalized ad-man or madman, or perchance a pervert who goes to the trouble of writing a shelf of books to rationalize his own hopelessly vicious tastes.

Nobody thinks of him as simply a guy who sees ugly gaps in the social nexus and builds gadgets to stitch them together, with motives no more or less devious than those of the inventor of the needle.

College didn't improve Jimmy's reputation except with a reluctant smidgin of sociologists who sometimes knew the difference between a workable device and a bejargoned dream. Like any young inventor Jimmy experimented as often and inevitably as he breathed, and anyone who experiments with society or any fraction of it is doing something a mite trickier than juggling barely subcritical masses of uranium-235. Some college boards don't like it when one freshman section learns twice as fast because of an unheard-of and presumably immoral student-instructor relationship, or when a faculty committee finally discovers a maddeningly smooth way of opposing the policies of the prexie. Some student advisors get indignant when a group of easy-to-manage apron-tied young neurotics form what they call a positive semi-brotherhood and soon become troublesome—that is, turn into men. Jimmy wasn't bailed or nailed as the inventor of any of these devices, he merely got the name of being a young squirt with an unfingerable trick for making his elders uncomfortable by giving them new slants on things.

At college Jimmy met a fellow student who was to be his bitterest and most single-minded enemy then and thereafter: Wilson Jervis Porter, later Attorney General of the United States. W. J. made an accurate estimate of Jimmy's importance earlier than anyone else, though his evaluation of Jimmy's motives was less than enlightened. He used his position as president of Jimmy's class, business manager of the football team, and editor of the student paper to tag Jimmy as a pinko, potential pervert and general under-miner of hallowed American institutions.

Jimmy wasn't in a position to refute W. J.'s attacks very effectively. Contrary to what some people might suspect Jimmy wasn't a Big Man On Campus or a natural leader or an office-grabber. Like most inventors he was a rather lonely person, spending so much time dreaming up handy man-to-man and girl-meets-boy gadgets that he had no opportunity to take personal advantage of them.

In the long run Jimmy Villon would have perfected gadgets to smooth and reality-tie the activities of college boards and student governments, but he quit college in his third year, to divide his time between bread-and-butter work for management-consultant and human-relationship firms that wanted results not impressive verbiage, occasional co-authorship of a scholarly paper with a social scientist who didn't mind sharing honors with a bright assistant, and his own ever-broadening research. He was perfecting his methods now—a combination of social statistics, psychophysics, cross-cultural indexing, and a generous dash of something very individual which it is hard to describe except as villonics. But contrary to W. J. and some of his other detractors he wasn't simply dreaming up ideas to suit the public fancy or digging out and modernizing social relationships from past cultures, he was inventing things just as surely as if he had been working with metals and plastic. As was said considerably later by Justice White, who wrote the sharply diverging minority opinion when the Supreme Court rejected the first batch of Jimmy's inventions as unpatentable: "If the invention of a device which clearly halves the divorce rate does not merit the description 'a flash of genius,' neither does the invention of anti-collision radar and it presumes we must thank a change in human nature for the reduction of traffic deaths by ninety percent!"

But whatever their status at the Patent Office, Jimmy's inventions were beginning to make themselves felt on a nationwide scale in such phenomena as the election upsets of 1964, the sharp decline in juvenile delinquency (coincident with the development of the semi-brotherhood gangs), the exchange-of-lives movement, the oldster-hoods, and the multi-families which licked a lot of urban problems from loneliness to baby-sitting and which were given their first shadowy legal recognition as a useful fiction in 1971.

Some very oddly assorted people and organizations ben-efitted from Jimmy's gadgets, for he paradoxically took after the whole tribe of artificers in not worrying much about the social consequences of his inventions. He saw people operating bumblingly, sketched out a self-perpetuating device that would let them operate smoothly, and then mostly forgot about the whole business, whether the smoothly-operating beneficiaries were a guild of technicians, Space Ventures Incorporated, the American Association of Psychosomatic Therapists, the Minute Maids of Columbia, or the Sons of the White Emperor.

However, this ethical blindness of Jimmy's, easily labeled opportunism, played an important part in the concerted attack on his work that began to develop and that was coordinated largely by W. J., now well on his road to the attorney-generalship. The old "Dreadful Motives" sign was underlined, spotlighted, wired for sound, and taped for broadcast. Jimmy was simultaneously accused of being a subversive and an arch-reactionary—as he himself put it, he was supposed to be propping up the tottering social framework only to knock it down in a more dramatic manner. In solemn terminology psychologists and psychiatrists claimed that Jimmy was trying to muscle in on their field, although Jimmy had often stated that he worked with the externals of people and was quite willing to leave to others the work of exploring and repairing the individual human mind. While the assorted lunatic fringes that at times seem to make up the whole fabric of society joyously joined together in leveling at Jimmy the age-old charges of communism and free love, the latter supposedly masquerading under the thin disguise of the multifamily, although the latter clearly had no reproductive or genetic function whatever and in spite of the obvious fact that no love is free even if much of it is worth the price.

Most of the accusations, whether made by religious cultists, cultural-determinist anthropologists, or the untiring

W. J., boiled down to this: Man cannot shape his social development, so true social inventions are impossible; any seeming social inventions must be plots, conspiracies, delusions and hoaxes. This line of reasoning attracted a wide following and for a time Jimmy could claim to be Public Enemy Number One. He was burned or run out of a number of towns in effigy, his research materials were cut off from him, several injunctions were issued against the operation of his presumably imaginary inventions, and with great fanfare a resolution to deport him was introduced in Congress. Jimmy was widely ostracized and all the letters of his last name gleefully pronounced.

It might be expected that Jimmy would escape from his predicament by some unexpected stroke of cleverness, but his vindication was as unmelodramatic and simple as one of his inventions—in fact the pendulum swung back and then stopped swinging exactly as Jimmy had predicted it would in *The Dialectic of Love and Hate*. The reasons were obvious: Jimmy's inventions had made him too many friends, those who were hottest against him had benefitted the most from them, and the chief weapon used against him was the very one a social inventor is best equipped to resist—social pressure!

As for W. J., he had to admit what the vehemence of his feelings proved and what Jimmy had known all along: that from the very beginning he had been Jimmy's semi-brother.

THE ADVENTURER

THE ONCOMING DARK was big, and he was little, yet he
stayed out in it, close to the door for safety. Something,
it might have been catbirds, made a rustling in the matted
blackness next door, where had once been a house, but now
only a pit with hunks of cemented brick hidden by rank weeds
and taller vegetation. Overhead the leaves of the wild cherry
stirred in the wind. In his nose was the smell of rain-washed
gravel and wet rotten wood, the kind that chunks off when
you kick a wooden sidewalk.

Out beyond the pit, where the street lights irked the darkness, was the town. Other boys lived there, and adults whose
clothes and faces confined a forceful unknown substance akin
to the darkness.

Soon his mother would come to the screen door, her face
a silhouette or rich blond shadows, and call him in to dinner. He wanted dinner and yet he wished that dinner would
not be ready too soon. He wished that dinner were always
almost ready.

Without getting up from the steps, he turned away from
the town and sent the Adventurer marching out into the

red-smudged west, where there were no street lights. Up and down across the old gravel-diggings went the Adventurer, past the rusted carcass of an antique car, through the sweet grass that grew on the ridges between the shallow cuttings. Something, perhaps a cat or rat, made a movement behind one of the sprawled fenders, and the Adventurer asked, "Who's that?" and, getting no answer, went on until he came to the little twisted woods. There he paused, looking back at Martin and the town, and, peering across the road to the decayed farm, in whose disused musty stable you could find great mysterious wooden implements and other devices, with iron attachments, for the tillage of crops and the control of animals. The wood was gray and dry, yet in places softly polished by hands that had gone away.

Then, driven by the urge that was without goal yet needed no explaining, the Adventurer plunged into the woods, holding out his hands to ward from his eyes the twigs that guarded the path. It was very dark in there, and hidden things challenged his passage without saying anything or even moving, yet he pressed onward along the twisting, ever downward creeping path, until he came out at the edge of the little swamp. The swamp was bigger now, and the sharp-edged sea-grass was taller and more sword-like than he remembered it. The sky was changed to a greenish gray, like the wax beads of the glossy-leafed bayberry bushes fringing the swamp. And creatures swam beneath the still surface of the brackish swamp-lake, making the lily pads stir.

Again he paused, looking back once more although the woods cut him off from Martin. Overhead he made out a sea hawk hurrying home, carrying in its claws something that writhed like a worm. Again he shoved onward, testing the ground with his feet for fear of bog holes.

THE ADVENTURER

Back on the porch steps, Martin watched the same sea hawk with its eel, as it doggedly beat toward some strong-built nest atop a thunder-stripped tree or telephone pole in the hills. It was darker now, and not easy to keep contact with the Adventurer, yet he continued to egg him onward, glorying in his power over distance and darkness.

In this same mood he had many times sent out the Adventurer. And he had also often put something of the Adventurer into little sticks and stones or marbles or lead soldiers, so that he could with his hands manoeuvre the Adventurer through vast hypothetical worlds symbolized by a few feet of floor or a few hillocks of boxed sand. Sometimes that meant splitting up the Adventurer to animate at once many units, which then fought with each other and were killed and buried. Yet their opposition to one another was not of much significance, but only their opposition to the vast and dangerous unknown realms which they explored. When he played with other boys, they put something of the unknown into the men they manoeuvred, though not enough to make them altogether alien.

The unknown was wonderfully frightening, with its great war that it kept across the sea and its exciting submarines that it hid under the sea. Sometimes there was a booming noise, which his father said came from the proving grounds, and once the west had been noise and flames all night when a place called a munitions work exploded. But mostly it kept the war to itself.

Meanwhile the Adventurer had come to an unfamiliar region, where great rocks made a jagged wall against the faintly glowing green sky. He climbed them, and found himself on the rim of a vast chasm. Across the chasm stretched a cable so thin that you could not see the further half of it.

Yet he knew at once he must cross by that rope. With only a keen glance at the darkness across and below, he swung out into the abyss hand over hand. Immediately those who had been following him came into plain view and shouted threateningly at him and waved their clenched fists angrily and cast missiles, which he dodged by swinging. Then one of them, more daring, swung out along the cable, and the rest followed.

Vast forms moved in the blackness below, thrusting wide, thousand-toothed jaws up at him on their long reptilian necks, almost near enough so that he could kick them. And ahead, on a little pinnacle of rock that rose in the center of the chasm was a great cat from the jungles of the unknown, which snarled and lashed out at the cable with its great claws.

He was almost in the middle now. Looking back he could see that his pursuers were overtaking him. And spying far ahead, he saw to his dismay that there were other enemies on the opposite rim of the chasm, and that one of them was sawing at the cable with a knife. At that moment, his hands touched a small, ugly-looking box bound tightly to the cable. The ticking that came from it told him that it was a time bomb, and the position of the hands on the dial told him that it was about to explode.

"Dinner's ready, Martin," called his mother through the screen, and he got up and went in, not bothered that he had to break contact with the Adventurer, because the Adventurer was exceptionally resourceful and had crossed the chasm many times before.

There was always something that caught you up a little as you entered the house, as if the air in it were the breath of a life, exhaled by the house and the things in it. For his father had built it all himself, from the locust foundation posts up. Martin remembered how he had been lifted up to see the roof shingled when he was very little. There had been a lot of bigger boys up there; later he realized that they must have been helping his father.

THE COMMUNICANTS

IN ALOOF, BREATH-CATCHING beauty, the central mass of the sky-scraper, its cross-section a gigantic plus sign, thrust upward to where the jet-driven traffic whispered through the night.

But at its terraced base were gathering the forces of a bitter and hysterical hate which might have shocked even the horror-calloused Twentieth Century.

There were only two figures at the focus of that hate—a man and a woman clad in softly flowing, darkishly gleaming synthetics. They had been backed up against a display-front in which, unheeded by the sullen crowd, a robot mannequin was parading costly garments with an every-recurrent nod and smile which the carefulest designing could not keep from looking like either a simper or a smirk.

Stoical patience and dark pride were apparent in the drawn faces of those two, but there was more than that—the signs of a frightening knowingness, as if they could see the unseen.

The ugly quarrel which had first drawn the crowd was still going on, but its significance had subtly changed. It had ceased to be a personal affair and had become the prelude to the unleashing of mob violence. The anger-shaky young man facing the two at bay seemed to sense this, and the confirming nods that his words elicited from the white, hate-contorted faces behind him made it obvious that he spoke for the mob.

"You dirty communicants! It's time something was done about your kind. Why don't you go ahead and try to deny that you invaded my wife's privacy, pried into her mind, undressed her? You don't dare, because I could tell from your faces what you were thinking. No matter how pure and innocent a woman is, she isn't safe from your kind. Your very thoughts sully her. Nothing's safe anymore from your filthiness!"

"Yes," a woman behind him chimed in hysterically. "Finding out peoples' secrets, then blackmailing them!"

"Or stealing their inventions, plagiarizing their creative ideas!"

"What about the fortunes you communicants got hidden away?" yapped a man at the edge of the crowd. "Anybody could make the right investments if he was a mind-reader."

"The Commonwealth's afraid to touch you. There aren't any laws against your crimes...yet!"

"Maybe we shouldn't wait for laws!"

"Go ahead and deny it," the young man repeated doggedly, edging forward. "You haven't answered me yet. Go ahead and deny it."

At last, with a shrug of proud resignation, the man backed against the display front spoke. His speech, though flawless, was strangely deliberate and studied. Unmistakably, he was not using his mother tongue.

"You are all acquainted with our assurances that we respect mental privacy, that we are pledged to derive no personal gain from our power, and that we keep close watch on each other to see that that pledge is kept. If you put no trust in our assurances, what use is there in my arguing?"

Angry jeers greeted the statement. The man's face changed. It was as if a mask of restraint, which had been kept in place with difficulty, were suddenly ripped from his features. Momentarily the crowd shrank back from what they saw.

"Do you think I'd concern myself with your cheap little minds?" he cried. "I have better things to do than accumulate mythical fortunes, blackmail fools, or pry into the vanities and boudoir secrets of an empty-headed matron!"

In the moment of silence following that outburst, a hoarse whisper was audible. "Did you see his face? They're devils!"

The man heard it and laughed bitterly.

But the woman standing beside him did not seem to hear it. At least, she did not heed it. She had stepped up onto the curb of the display front and was peering across the crowd. Her eyes noted, but did not linger on, the backs of two Commonwealth Police. Eventually they found what they were searching for.

Across the lanes of traffic slowly trundling along at urban surface speeds, stood a gray-haired couple in evening clothes. With them was a spindly, red-headed boy. The boy kept pointing to the crowd. He seemed to be making some sort of wild plea. The gray haired man was shaking his head. He had the boy by the wrist.

A puzzled look came into her eyes, as if she ought to recognize the boy, but didn't.

Stung by fresh accusations, the man was once more lashing out at the crowd. "Steal your thoughts? I only wish there were some way to shut them out! If you only knew how stupid and petty they were! How naked and threadbare! The monotony of them is enough to drive a man crazy! And as for planting my thoughts in your minds, I wish I could! A few intelligent ones!"

She thought: "Watch out, Greer. You're letting their hate get you. You're reflecting it, like a mirror."

He thought back: "Grayl, let me alone! I'm going to tell them off, once and for all. I won't have another chance. Feel their thoughts, Grayl! This time they're going to kill."

She was watching the boy. He had suddenly jerked away from the gray-haired man and ducked into a snub-nosed, black coupe, out of which a parking attendant had just stepped. Reckless of regulations, the coupe swung through the traffic in an U-turn. The gray-haired man had stopped at the curb and was shouting something and shaking his fist.

The crowd was surging forward again. The young man who had been so loud in defence of his wife's honor, finally struck out wildly. Greer caught and pinioned his arms.

"You don't care about your wife!" There was something terrible about the way Greer ground out the words. "You're only angry because you know I can see how cowardly and indecisive and contemptible you are inside." Greer's voice rose. "That's why all of you hate the communicants. You can't bear to think that anyone should be able to catch a glimpse of the cheap hypocrisies and nasty private daydreams you treasure up in your selfish egos! Each one of you has always known just how contemptible he was. But each of you hugged that knowledge to yourself. Now the secret's out! Would you like me to tell it? Who'll be first!"

She thought: "That's deliberate suicide, Greer." She felt the hatred of the mob lick out at her, like an unclean flame. A woman clawed at her face, tore at her dress. A dozen hands were grabbing at Greer. Animal snarls.

But from the back of the mob yells of a different sort were coming. With a cushiony jolt, the black coupe had nosed up onto the terrace. It shoved into the mob, its raindrop nose ramming gently. There was a general panicky scramble for safety. The red-haired boy was at the controls. Grayl was sure now that she had never seen him before. He kicked open the door and in an excited, high-pitched voice yelled, "Get in!" Greer was still fighting two men. He was deaf to Grayl's urgent thought. He knocked one down. The other fled. Grayl had to pull him into the coupe. He seemed dazed, sullenly indifferent to rescue.

Then, with ever-mounting acceleration, the coupe lurched back into traffic and, before it had passed two skyscrapers, broke something more than the speed laws, by skimming up into the night.

Behind, whistles skirled. The Commonwealth Police had at last gone into action. The mob collected itself, buzzing like a disturbed hive of bees. While in the display front, the robot mannequin, with the inevitable simper and smirk, opened wide a negligee, to show the latest fashion in nightgowns.

INSIDE THE COUPE the faint drumming of the jets was a rumbling pulse. Grayl could feel the tautness of the boy's skimpy muscles, the almost spasmodic intensity of his concentration. She told him: "Traveling at this level you'll be picked up in two minutes."

"He replied: "I know. Wait."

"I see. You're heading for the Old City."

"Yes."

"Good idea."

Grayl braced herself. The coupe banked around the gaunt, fluted column of a skyscraper. Through the bright windows she glimpsed people. Suddenly flat roofs, cramped closely together, were below them. The Old City—a luxury area in mid-Twentieth Century, now a low rental district waiting to be demolished and replaced with generously-spaced skyscrapers.

The coupe slowed, coasted down into an almost-empty street. There was a lurch as the streamlined under-shield was retracted from the wheels. With a sickening jolt the coupe landed. The boy sent it surging forward under surface power. He turned at the next corner and went on for a few blocks—at random, Grayl sensed. Then, with something that sounded like a sob, he brought it to a stop and slumped back, trembling.

Grayl told him soothingly: "You did a beautiful job. These new atomotor coupes are hard to handle."

He was still shaking. She touched his hand. It was like ice.

After a moment she observed: "Strange that we should never have been in contact before. What chapter do you belong to?"

"Chapter? I don't know what you mean."

"But surely… Why did you rescue us then?"

His answer came with a torrent of emotion: "Because they were going to kill you. I knew it. And you two were so fine, and you were facing them so bravely. Suddenly I realized that you were my kind—the ones I had always been looking for, the ones I had given up hope of ever finding. I just had to do what I did."

He looked up at her then, halting amazement in his pinched, tear-stained face. His shrill voice broke the silence.

"We've been talking! We've been talking together—but we haven't said a word!"

She was smiling at him tenderly. He could tell that she now understood what to him was still a mind-wrenching confusion.

"That's right, Perc."

"But Grayl, how do you know my name?"

"How do you know mine, Perc?"

He felt her gentle compassion, like a caress. "Don't you see, Perc? They've been hiding the truth from you. You're a communicant."

"But the communicants are bad… Only that can't be right, if you're communicants. But…" He stopped. He was shaking again. "Would you mind talking? It all comes too fast the other way. I can't get things straight."

"Certainly, Perc. Words do help to make thoughts more definite. You had Gorton's Disease, didn't you—and a pinealectomy?"

"I don't know. I was very sick a year ago, and they operated on my brain, if that's what you mean. I began to really see into people then, to feel what they were feeling. I told my father and mother about it, but they were angry and said I must hide it and never mention such things."

"They were right, Perc, in their way." He felt her weary disillusionment, and it chilled him. "Communicants aren't very popular now."

"But I still don't understand. Communicants read minds. I don't. I just see people's thoughts in their faces, of hear them in their voices, or…"

"Of course. You project them, like any other sensations. You don't think of my face as a visual pattern on your retina. You think of it as being out here, where I am. It's the same with the telepathic images you get from my mind."

"But what did my being sick and the operation have to do with it?"

"Everything. Telepathy was discovered purely by accident in the course of combatting Gorton's Disease—hypertrophy of the pineal gland. Man has always been potentially telepathic, but the pineal gland acted as a nullifier. Many simple, primitive animals *are* telepathic—communal unicellular organisms are a striking example. But in the middle stages of evolution telepathy prevented the development of individuality—it ceased to favor survival. As a result, nullifier organs were developed. But, potentially, telepathy persisted. As soon as his pineal gland is removed, a person becomes telepathic."

The boy sat hunched in thought. A troubled frown made more prominent a blue vein in his white forehead. From the gloom passers-by stared at the coupe. The old street was like a deep slot in darkness.

Finally he looked up at Grayl perplexedly. "But why doesn't everyone become a communicant then, if that's all there is to it? Don't they realize how wonderful it could be?"

Her reply was bitter. "Do you know the pinealectomy mortality, even with the new technique? Forty per cent, though it's much lower with infants. Who'd take such a chance, unless he had Gorton's Disease? Besides, there are...prejudices."

"Why, Grayl?"

"Well, for one thing, a few of the first communicants actually did use their power to swindle people in various ways. But that was stopped when the communicants organized themselves. Now we keep watch on each other, telepathically, so that communicants are much more effectually hindered from anti-social action than any other segment of the world community."

"But in that case, why do people hate you... Us... so terribly? That crowd..."

Greer had not spoken a word. Now Grayl sensed his locked thoughts uncoil, like serpents striking. They frightened her. She sensed the boy quail from them.

Why do they hate us? Simply because we can see their

private shame and nastiness. Weren't your father and mother mighty cautious about what they thought when they were near you? Wasn't everyone suspicious? Of course! They hate us because we can see their minds and they can't see ours. They won't believe us when we tell them that a sensitivity like ours constitutes a terrible responsibility and a killing burden. There are about a hundred thousand of us communicants, and we're pretty widely distributed—Gorton's Disease isn't geographically localized. Enough of us so that our combined telepathic sensitivities cover the whole Earth. Understand what that means, son? It means that if I concentrate, and if I contact other telepaths, who in turn contact others, I can—dimly and foggily of course—listen to the whole world think!

"Bad enough, son, to know that people hate and suspect you. But that's nothing to actually feeling that hate, night and day, a steady flow you can never quite shut out. Bad enough to know that there are cruel and vicious people. But to wake up in the middle of the night and find yourself thinking their thoughts... Or to listen in on people who literally and simply want to destroy the world—I've had that experience, and they weren't all in asylums, either. You've been shielded, son, and you haven't really learned how to use your powers, but when you do..."

Grayl thought: "This is unworthy of you, Greer. You're just trying to frighten him." Greer ignored her, and from the boy she caught the thought: "No, I want him to go on. I want to hear everything now."

"Take the next war, son. The Elwood atomotor and the Elwood process have provided us for the first time in history with a means of directly converting atomic energy into mechanical power or instantaneous destructive force. Poor old Elwood's a kind of pacifist—I listened in on his mind once.

He released his discoveries to the whole world with the naive idea that that would prevent war. Now he sees that it will only make war more destructive, and he's eating his heart out over it.

"The point is, everyone knows that the next war will be a terrible one, if it comes. But only the communicants have to watch it coming, step by inevitable step, have to feel the minds of the Commonwealth statesmen falter and temporize at the critical moments, while the leaders of the Confederation lose their normal realism and being to think they can get away with anything."

"But that's just where the communicants can help," the boy interrupted eagerly. "The communicants can avert wars, prevent crime, do away with misunderstanding."

"Right! That's what we all thought. But it doesn't work out that way. Our kind of testimony is not admissible in a court of law; there's no provision for telepathic evidence. The government offices won't have anything to do with us, although in some cases we've offered our services. The thing's too big for them. All they can see is the possibility of information leakages. The War Office has even started a big research on thought screens—a research that's almost certain to prove futile, since they won't use communicants on it.

"Everywhere we turn it's the same. Uniformly negativistic reaction to any proposals we may make. Blind, unshakable prejudice. And as blind and unshakable a hate. Do you know that the government is contemplating a measure that would place all communicants in isolated concentration camps? Do you know that all over the world people are dying of Gorton's Disease, because most hospitals have stopped operating for it? Do you know that they're already begun to lynch communicants in the Confederation? Do you know that they're holding mass-meetings against us, tonight, in this city? I don't have to tell you about the hate behind those actions. You can feel it, here and now."

Grayl felt the boy wince. "What you say is true, Greer," she thought, "But what use is there in harping on it, unless you want to drive us all as mad as the world is?" She reached out with her mind, seeking to contact some communicant whose mind was not tainted with despair. Surely all of them couldn't be like Greer and herself, fatalistically anticipating doom. But her determination was unequal to the task, and she gave it up as soon as she had begun. She felt the world's hate like a dirty, impenetrable curtain around the coupe. The gloom of the Old City vibrated with it.

Greer continued inexorably: "Communicants are directly aware of psychological trends. Day by day, moment by moment, I've felt the hate grow, like water piling up behind a weakened dam. War scares slowed it a little, by dividing peoples' emotions. Yesterday's public reiteration by the communicants of their stand actually hastened it. Now the critical moment is at hand, when the dam breaks and the hate floods forth. Can't you feel it? I told you how I could listen to the world think. I'm listening to it now." Grayl sensed mind-racking madness in his thoughts. In the light from the control panel his face was a mask of evil suffering. "Tune your minds to mine," he commanded harshly, "and feel it. Feel it!"

Grayl felt his mind close round hers and the boy's. There was something blasphemous about it. The minds of Earth compressed into one. A billion thoughts superimposed upon each other, cancelling out their differences, leaving only what was the same in each. Hate.

Hysterically, the boy began to scream.

THE FEELER

ALL AT ONCE Max Hynes began to feel acutely thirsty—
just for water, not for alcohol. He shouldn't have, since
he'd had a cool and satisfying glassfull not ten minutes before.
He wondered, with a freezing premonition, whether this was
the first symptom of the umpteenth of the mysterious diseases
(both somatic and psycho) that had put hiatuses in his life
and vacuum in his pocketbook, and at first rouses his wife's
sweet passion to take care of something, but lately completely
bored her. This large cuddlesome creature was sulking on
the pneumo couch with her neck at an uncomfortable angle
and her fashionably zig-zag bands almost in her eyes and her
whole being expressing that touchingly universal plea: "I want
somebody to make me do something."

Max inspected Myna's solid, Junoesque figure interestingly indenting the pneumo couch and still felt thirsty just
for water. He thought: *perhaps—Freud forbid!—I'm regressing
to oral eroticism.*

But after all, he wasn't thirsty for milk, or molecular baby
formula colored with harmless vegetable dyes, just water. He
looked around the rest of the room: his reading tapes, Myrna's

antique phonograph—the latter playing for the second time the topmost of a stack of rare circular records she hadn't the energy to get up and turn over. Nothing in the room gave him a clue to his thirst, and he had to admit he could hardly expect it to.

He checked his memory. He could distinctly visualize himself pushing the button that gently boosted him out of his easy chair. He could likewise recall going to the kitchen, telling the light to turn on, commanding the water to run, ordering it to stop when the glass was filled to a precise inch from the brim. Two drops of the careless water had splashed his bony wrist.

But had it happened ten minutes ago, last night, or two months back? He unhappily realized he couldn't be absolutely sure. His memory had been treacherous lately: smilingly handing him things that happened years ago, or to other people, or to characters in reading tapes, or that weren't due to happen yet, if ever. Not often, but enough to be worrisome. Here, possibly, was one more example.

Any rate, he was deucedly thirsty. Why, he asked himself, don't they invent something that levitates a drink of water to you without all this fuss of going to the kitchen and talking to the faucet? Wearily he fingered a convenient button. The easy chair slowly straightened itself into an almost-upright resting frame. He did the last six inches of the work of getting up, and headed kitchenwards.

On his way, being a thoughtful husband, he turned over the stack of records.

The commanded water purled down his throat in artistic gushes and trickles, rippling over and around his tongue, caressing his soft pallet.

He felt as thirsty as ever. Bone dry.

THE FEELER

He tongued the remaining bits of water in his mouth, felt them squish and spread as he rubbed them in. It didn't do a bit of good.

Here it comes again, he told himself with a resigned horror he hardly had the strength to summon up. *I've got hydrophilia, as they'll probably christen it* (Max had already had five diseases unknown to medical science). *Eight more full courses of good old aCTH and the new nerve drugs. Seventeen more months of pouring forth my session-worn little soul to a psychoanalytic listen-and-probe machine that will accidentally be geared to moron-speed every second session. And me eternally parched until they manage trial-and-error wise to nudge the right enzyme of complex.*

For a horrid moment he imagined himself bulging with water like a victim of the medieval funnel-torture—and *still* thirsty. Max had an exceptionally nasty imagination that he didn't like at all.

All these impending horrors and bothers subway-crushing themselves in his mind, he headed back toward the living room. But before he did so, being an exceedingly, even automatically thoughtful husband, he filled a glass of water for his wife. He also commanded the refrigerator to toss out two cubes, and caught them in the glass with hardly a splash. Myna probably would disdain it, but what the heck. Got to be courteous, even when nervous systems collapse.

Momentarily absorbed by the new fear that his throat was ridden with deliquescent germs capable of stealing every drop of water, he drank. Too, he had some lurking fear as to whether the clear stuff coming from the tap was actually water. Though it had tasted like water, except for not quenching his thirst.

When he offered the glass to Myna abstractedly she accepted it with an air of "Oh well, if you insist" or "I don't care if I do." Then she drank it down, tilting it real high, so that the cubes nestled against her stylishly green upper lip.

Instantly, Max felt completely refreshed. He gazed at Myna with a certain horror. He ran his tongue all around his mouth, inside and out of his teeth, rather desperately searching for dryness, trying to revive it, but encountered only contented moistness. He swallowed and it felt just slushy.

He was left with the bare fact: Myna's drinking had cured his thirst.

Max tottered to the resting frame and buttoned it for "Utter Slump."

Max wouldn't have been so devastated by this mildly peculiar coincidence, if it hadn't been for a number of suspiciously similar episodes during the past few days, especially that of the yearned-for twenty-five cents.

To begin with, there was his new-found trouble-spotting ability at the office. Lately, when the three-o'clock *Wanderlust* (that common heritage of all white-collar workers, driving them to the liquid dispenser or relaxo-room, or merely trivial errands that are excuses for chatting) had hit the place, he had found himself wandering about unhappily until he sensed he had discovered some colleague who had real troubles to unload, not just boredom to enjoy in company. It was as if at those times he had an unhappiness-radar inside him. Then, as he listened to his targets pour out their troubles, his own misery would clarify and generally vanish.

But this was nothing to build theories on, since most of the people at the office were bored and moody, especially around three-o'clock, due in large part to the nature of their employment. Max Hynes belonged to a service that counseled counseling services. In the indecisive, self-mistrusting modern world, counseling services had mushroomed. There were services that offered to come in and straighten out your personnel problems, your personal problems, your advertising, promotion, and extraterrestial problems, to shlock up your business generally. Whether you published reading-tapes or projecto-books, whether you rented sitter-robots or mechanical carrier pigeons, whether you sold TV sets, earplugs, throwaway paper dresses, sex hormones or temporary-sterility tablets, there was a counseling service that would come in when sales fell off and office set-ups went murky.

They would psych the office-boy, fire Mr. Wilolset, promote Miss Wang, send the boss on a rest-trip to the moon, put noiseless tires on the filing robots, do a spot-check of Martian customer-reactions, suggest a series of flasher-yowler advertisements, present you with enough microstatted curves to construct three glamor girls and seven BEMs, clap you on the back several times, and then depart with a big grin and a bigger check, leaving you feeling, if not reassured, at least remarkably shaken up.

Naturally, from time to time, these counseling services suffered from the same disease it was their business to cure. Hence the super-service in which Max Hynes functioned as a human relay.

But, as the filing-robot supervisor once put it trenchantly, "Who shall counsel the counselors of the counselors?" Since no such service as yet existed in human society, Max's office mates were regularly afflicted with periods of vast gloom and self-mistrust.

THE WRONG TRACK

AFTER A MOMENT'S hesitation, like a surly animal suddenly roused from slumber, the timeclock's internal jaws champed on his card. Without losing a step, he snatched it out, flicked it into the swingshift Inspection rack, bared his teeth at the green ghost of Bataan who sternly counselled against absenteeism, lit his cigarette, and dodged out into the camouflage-roofed, dirt-paved night.

The bluish floodlights sucked all color from the hurrying array of shirts and sweaters, overalls and slacks. By sticking to the shadowed walls, where one met only an occasional tardy graveyard worker sprinting for his clock, by keeping to the inside of a dark parked truck loaded with high-looming wing-sections and pieces of cowling, he managed to keep clear of the main stream.

But in a minute he was wedged in the midst of the gray tide which surged between the glaring gate and the huge scoreboard which recorded the number of bombers that could have been built with the work-hours lost last month.

Another minute and his poised fingers were flipping open his lunchbox to reveal the mess of eggshells, sandwich fragments, and wadded wax paper which he might just as well have disposed of inside the plant.

Then the policewoman's eyes flickered up to the next badge and he was outside in the relative dark, free at last to feel alone, to organize his hates, to savor the churning in his guts and the ringing in his ears which the drop-hammers, grinders, and saws had produced with contemptuous ease.

He headed past the warming motorcycles down the black side-aisle of the parking lot. Already cars were coming to life under the acres of feather-fretted chicken-wire. Headlights were swinging. First-aways were gunning their motors, racing for the exit. After mistaking only two other cars for it, he spotted Ernie's, retraced his steps, and climbed in between the heavy-armed blonde from final assembly and the old man from jig-crib whose name he didn't remember.

"Guess Olga'll be the one to hold us up tonight," remarked Ernie with a disarming chuckle. The old man started to grunt, but switched to a relieved sigh as Olga swung into the front seat, ducking to slip her lunch box under her legs.

Without wasting any time, Ernie shoved them into a gap left in the center-aisle stream, when a blue coupe momentarily faltered.

As they headed away from the plant, through dark streets and gradually thinning traffic, conversation highlighted the night's salient events, paused for the customary jokes and digs, soared briefly when Olga got rid of her ire against a cantankerous foreman, settled down to victory gardens.

George, comfortably bolstered in back seat center, took no part. As anonymous as a man in an eight-car commuters' train, he sat observing the dark heaving landscape of his mind. It was too early for it to have produced even definite thoughts, let alone words, which of course could not be uttered here in any case. He just lay back and felt.

After they'd dropped the others and it was no longer possible to talk about tomatoes, Ernie asked him if he was still doing any acting. He stilled his curiosity with a couple of vague remarks.

They drew up at the corner. As he swung out, Ernie warned him, "I'll be going in about ten minutes ahead of time tomorrow. Have to see about my gas ration."

George nodded, grinned like a skull, said, "Night."

He dropped his lunchbox on the table and walked softly into the dark bedroom.

He said, "I feel horrible."

The surge of the Pacific four blocks away sounded like a load of coal being dumped on a hollow sidewalk and scattering. It blotted out the thin wail of traffic. Down the street a dog howled and from downstairs one of Mrs. Cleveland's Scotties yapped a challenge.

He walked over to the bed and put his hand on Connie's shoulder.

"I feel horrible," he explained.

"Wha...?" She shivered and turned over.

"I feel horrible," he repeated.

"Oh. Was it especially bad tonight, darling?"

He stood up. "Of course. But that's not the point. It's just that I have the feeling, I don't know, that everything is so wrong."

She murmured agreement. "Come on to bed. You're tired." Her hand groped for his.

He stepped back. "...so completely and utterly wrong. Everything. No, I couldn't possibly sleep. When I think of the mistakes the world made. This war. The stupid, premeditated mistakes. The mistakes I've made, quitting my acting, grabbing at a war job, trapping myself. It's just one godawful mess. And there's no way out of it."

The springs creaked as she sat up, groped for a bathrobe.

"Shall I make you something to eat?"

"No, I'm not hungry. I brought half my lunch home. It's still in the box."

"Do you want a drink?"

"I don't know. Do you?"

"Yes."

"All right." But he made no move toward the kitchen. "God, I feel horrible," he said.

"Isn't there something I can do?"

"No."

"Isn't there…"

"No."

"Oh, darling, I can't bear to watch you be so miserable and not be able to do anything about it."

"I have to tell someone about it. There's nothing you can do about it, but you can help me just by listening." As he spoke, he walked toward the bed.

"I feel so out of touch with you, though. A thousand miles away."

"You shouldn't. Don't you see, I'm trying to tell you everything so we'll be close together. It's because I love you that I have to share this with you. I love you so completely that…"

He felt the touch of her hand and jerked away, wincing. His compressed eyeballs smudged the darkness with red. He peered through it, from the other side of the room, toward the bed.

Twice the Pacific rumbled up the beach, starting way off in one direction, ending in the opposite.

"Aren't you going to get the drinks?" she asked.

"In a little while. When I stop feeling so wrought-up."

Bare feet thudded rapidly across the floor. He put up his arm as if to ward off an attack, but the steps continued to the kitchen and the light went on.

In a moment he was taking the bottle out of her hand as she reached it down from the shelf.

"I'll make them," he said. "You don't have to."

She darted to the icebox, opened it, jerked at the frozen tray. He followed her.

"Let me," he said. "I didn't want you to bother."

[Ed: *possible page missing*]

There were rapid steps on the outside stairs. Connie broke off and stared at the door.

"You see what's happened now?" said George. "Mrs. Cleveland's heard you."

Connie kept looking.

The door shook under a heavy pounding. Then, through it, a rich, heavy voice: "Here's a knocking indeed. If a man were porter of hell-gate, he should have old turning the key."

Knock, knock, knock, knock, knock.

"Who's there, in the name of Beelzebu—bu—bu—bu—bub?"

Connie's eyes went to George, then back to the door. Her mouth formed, "Get rid of him!" She darted into the bedroom.

George shouted, "Come on in, Martin!" at the door, then ran after Connie, shutting the bedroom door after him.

She was snatching at things on her dressing table, knocking them off.

"What's the matter, Connie?" George whispered. "Why are you acting this way?"

"That idiot! Coming here at this time of night!"

"Shh! He can hear you."

"As if I cared! What does he think this place is—a beer joint, that he can wander in any time of night? You've got to get rid of him."

"I can't do that. Connie, stop acting this way."

"I'll scream."

"If you do, I'll murder you."

"Your friends have got the most impossible manners of any people I know. Artist!"

The knocking had stopped, but the monologue from Macbeth had come nearer. George stepped back. "I'm going out to see him," he said. "When you get ready, you come out too."

He hurried into the living room, again shutting the door behind him. Martin looked up from the photograph, where he was setting a record. He grinned. White skin, small eyes, broad face, and short red hair made the grin clownlike, despite his handsomeness.

"Was it so late, friend, ere you went to bed, that you do lie so late?" He demanded, scowling.

Then, picking up George's drink and tipping the remaining third of it down his throat, he answered himself, "Faith sir, we were carousing to the second cock." Then, relaxing, "Good morrow, worthy thane."

"How are the rehearsals going?" George asked.

"Pretty well. Where's Connie?"

"I think she'll be out in a minute."

Martin let down the needle and they listened to the first bars of Schubert's Unfinished.

"How do you like playing Macbeth?" George asked.

He expected a soliloquy in reply. Instead Martin said. "All right. It's really your part, though, old man."

"Nonsense. I'd like to do something in the play, of course. Banquo, maybe. But with this damn job…"

Martin looked at him over the glass. "Sure you wouldn't like to play Macbeth?" he asked.

"I want to see you play it, and no one else."

"But you see, I'm not so sure…"

"What's the matter, anyway?"

Martin looked at the bedroom door. Connie marched in. She'd put on a housecoat. George braced himself, but she merely went over and sat down on the sofa. She didn't say anything.

Martin nodded at her, looked at his glass, then at both of them.

"Well, the fact is," he said, "I've been drafted."

"But you're 4-F."

"Was."

"You mean at this last examination…?"

"Yes. They decided my heart murmur wasn't so serious. Yes, I know, I told you it would be a breeze. But I've got my papers and may be called up any day."

"That's terrible."

Martin nodded.

Connie had been looking at him coldly. "What are you going to do?" she asked.

Martin blew out his breath thoughtfully.

"You'll have time for the play, of course?" George prompted.

Martin shrugged. "I don't know. I mean I don't know if I'll stick with the play even if I have time."

"But you're in the middle of rehearsals. You wouldn't quit now."

Martin's eyes narrowed to slits. There was also melodrama in his outjutting lower lip and open mouth.

"Look," he said slowly. "I'm no idealist like you are and I don't give a damn for my word. I've done my share of cheating and I'm not sorry for it. I think the war's a godawful mess. I think the guys who drafted me into it are a bunch of white-haired bastards who would send their own mothers out to be shot if it would safeguard their interests and they could do it quietly. But I'll be damned if I'm going to let them get me down. What I'm going to have in the days of weeks left me is a good time, one hell of a good time. If the play fits in, okay. If it doesn't, nuts."

TRAP

PERIL TO THE Master!

That was Kennishaw's first thought on coming to himself. It dwarfed all others, striding like a giant through the tortured, murky confusion of his mind. It drowned out the messages of his senses. It filled to bursting the channels of his emotions with an anxiety that was all the more terrible because *he did not know what the danger was.* It beat against the walls of his memory, demanding an answer to that question—hammered against the ominous black sphere that projected into his consciousness but refused to become a part of it.

Peril to the Master! Kennison's body quailed and writhed under the merciless whiplash of that thought. It was more than if a man had learned secretly but with absolute certainty that the world would end tomorrow. It was as if a profoundly religious individual had found out, and seen indisputable proof of it, that the cosmos-ruling god whom he revered was some-how—unimaginably perhaps but still somehow—threatened with eternal extinction.

Kennishaw's mind groped wildly for telepathic contact with the Master's, sought by the very intensity of his thinking

FRITZ LEIBER

to attract the Master's attention to him, prayed to the Master to relieve him of his frightful burden, achieved—nothing.

In the extremity of his emotion, Kennishaw clawed and bit—and realized only then that it was earth that was under his hands and between his teeth, that he was lying prone on hard, bare ground.

Very slowly, very cautiously he lifted his head, muddied saliva trailing down unnoticed and staining the high collar of his unadorned gray tunic. All his senses were strainingly alert now for immediate danger, not on his own account, for he was a creature of no consequence, but because his continued existence had become of importance to the Master.

For it had suddenly come to him that, given only a little time, he would be able to still the confusion of his thoughts and penetrate the darkness of his memory, discover what peril it was that threatened the Master, and warn him. There was something strange about Kennishaw's sudden absolute assurance that he would be able to accomplish all these things, but he was not aware of the strangeness. The vastness of his responsibility now awakened in him only a kind of emotional intoxication, terrible but wonderful.

Tensing himself, drawing up his legs a little, ready to spring or crouch or roll—whichever should be demanded—he looked around.

Out from him, as far as the eye could see, stretched a flat, featureless gray wasteland, on which a blinding sun beat hotly from a sky of hurtful blue.

That wasteland struck Kennishaw as unnatural. There was in its very lifelessness the suggestion that titanic, all-trampling powers had battled there and might soon battle again. It looked as if it had been *beaten* flat.

TRAP

Stupidly Kennishaw's mind fumbled for the explanation he knew was within easy grasp.

Then he looked over his shoulder and, from the crouching position he had gradually assumed, instantly threw himself flat, trying to merge into the earth, to make his tunic and leggings indistinguishable parts of the landscape. But his head remained craned back at a painful angle and his white-ringed eyes still stared.

Only a few hundred yards away the inky walls began their outward and upward curving rise from the limitless gray scar of the wasteland. Like some fateful planetoid come down to perch on Earth, it reared itself there, obscuring a full eighth of the sky—a huge black globe, firmly bedded in the wasteland but with the greater portion above ground.

Its blackness was absolute. Of the ocean of sunlight that beat against it, no ray returned to hint at texture of three-dimensional form. It was perceptible only as an absence. Save for the oval shadow it cast, it might have been a great disk-shaped hole in reality.

To Kennishaw it was as if the ominous black sphere projecting into his consciousness had acquired a gigantic outward counterpart.

He knew there was a connection between the two, and that therein lay the key to the Master's danger.

Without warning, a tongue of dazzling energy licked out from the upper portion of the sphere, missed him by a matter of feet, pasted him flatter still with a burning blast of displaced air, churned to foamy dust the gray soil a few yards beyond, then flickered out with a thundering crackle as the displaced air returned.

Deafened, his retinal field seared across by a flaming after-image, Kennishaw lunged shakily to his feet, reeled forward those few yards, and dove through the dust cloud down into the sloping pit the energy-tongue had scooped.

Hot, powdery ash closed over him, tormented his gasping lungs, gave no handhold. Frantically he struggled, like an ant in an ant-lion's funnel as he slid, rolled, sank. Then it all heaved under and behind him, as a second energy-tongue struck the spot where he had originally been lying. Impact, transmitted through a colloid of dust and air, shook him to the bone, irresistibly lifted him in a slow somersault, hurled him to the pit's soft bottom. On him, cascades of ash settled, showing weight at last.

As hot, choking death closed down, his feelings were solely those of tortured self-accusation. He had failed the Master.

His flailing arm struck jagged solidity. He groped, found it again, this time with both hands. A thick, curving surface, unevenly broken off, set immovably in earth. And, underneath it, the suggestion of *openness*.

The weight of the dust grew momently greater as the sustaining air oozed upward out of it. It packed. As he strove to pull himself toward the jaggedness, he was stopped.

But the thought of the Master's peril went screaming down his nerves to lash his muscles into a final effort. One inch, then another, and another, through thick, suffocating dark. The jaggedness scraped his face, dug into his shoulder. The dust clung to his ankles like great hands. He writhed around, changed his grip, got better leverage, slithered through.

He slipped down a short incline of dust, reached another solidity beneath him, crawled weakly along it until he had gotten away from the worst of the heat and dust, then drew a breath that was still dust-laden and began to cough convulsively.

Still coughing, eyes still closed, he groped around him, felt curving solidity below, to either side, and, after getting to his feet, above.

TRAP

Of course! He was in one of the old tunnels. In seeking to destroy him, the Others had opened for him a way of escape.

Still coughing, he started forward as fast as he dared, feeling his way.

It was coming back now. He had been one of a large party sent by the Master to explore the old tunnels and determine if they could still be used as an avenue of attack against the Others. Their progress had been highly successful until they reached the neighborhood of the great black sphere that was the Others' fortress, where something—a gas, a ray, a psionic field—had snuffed out consciousness.

A memory-gap then, until he had awakened lying faced down on the gray wasteland.

But something must have happened in between, else why that hammering certainty that the Master was in danger?

Doubtless he had been taken prisoner, had probably even been transported inside the sphere, had learned of the Master's peril, had managed to escape—and in the very act of escaping had his memory wiped clean of all that had happened in the sphere.

Perhaps the field walling the sphere interfered with the escape of thought. Yes, that seemed likely, since one of its purposes was to shield the Others from the Master's telepathic influencings.

But if memories were sponged out by passage through the field, how could he hope to warn the Master?

A fierce surge of blind confidence answered that question for Kennishaw. He *knew* the Master was in danger. And somewhere in his subconscious the details survived. Given time, he could extract them.

Given time... Time must be paramount. A minute's unnecessary delay on his part...

Concussion rocked the corridor—from ahead. The tip of a burrowing energy-tongue illuminated the tunnel with ghastly brilliance, then flicked off in a chaos of descending earth.

The Others were blocking the tunnels, dealing with him like a mole.

But the momentary glare had shown him the opening of a side-tunnel a few paces ahead. He plunged into it, forcing his shaky legs into a run, his outstretched hand brushing the wall for a guide. He passed by the mouths of two intersecting tunnels tending in the same direction as the one he had left. He wanted to go in that direction, but they were too close to the first for safety. They might come within range of the Others' random probing.

When he found the fourth he turned into it, ran until he had to stop.

As he crouched panting, he began to take stock. The scraping his face had gotten was superficial. The wound in the shoulder felt deeper, but there didn't seem to be much blood. The effects of head and concussion were more difficult to determine. He felt sick and aching, certain areas of skin were painful to the touch and there were intermittent pains suggestive of organic injury. But that didn't matter so long as he could continue to function until his mission was completed.

He wiped dust from his eyes. The after-images ebbed to a greenish haze. He could begin to make out the faint whitish glow coming from the tubular walls. That was as it should be. He looked around for a hieroglyph identifying the corridor, found none in his vicinity. He felt a sudden wave of weariness.

Peril to the Master! The ever-recurring thought was like a goad, driving him up and on, but for the moment he purposely resisted it. He tried to relax his mind, make it a blank, so that the missing memories would have a chance to float up into consciousness. But the black bubble would not burst, although there was the suggestion that its walls were thinning. Just a little more time...

"Hear me, Master," Kennishaw prayed. "Let your globe-girdling mind take note of me. Let your spirit enfold and guide me. Grant me the boon of direct communion. O Master, hear me."

Kennishaw paused expectantly, his mind an empty, quivering screen for any thought the Master might choose to project. There came a feeling of peace and security, a sense of purpose in things, like the reassuring touch of great ghostly fingers. But nothing more.

Undiscouraged, Kennishaw set out once more down the tunnel. True, direct telepathic communion would have relieved him of his responsibility, for surely the Master could probe his small mind in an instant, but it was too much to hope for. The great mass of mankind never experienced it—they knew only the Master's general guidance, non-individualized, such as Kennishaw had felt after his prayer. With billions of minds to—

He began to pray.

He scrambled up and continued his flight, this time at a steady jog calculated to husband strength and postpone exhaustion.

Time passed. A kind of peace came to Kennishaw. There was something hypnotic about the softly glimmering tubular corridor, like treading the path of a search-beam through dark space. Something soothing about the rhythmical clop-clop of his sandals, making him forget the small jolt of pain each step sent through him. His consciousness of the Master's peril no longer filled him with anxiety. He was unshakably confident that, when the critical moment came, the black bubble in his mind would burst and he would remember the details of the danger.

He became aware of the Master's psychic field enfolding and cradling him.

BOOM, BOOM, BOOM!

AT MIDNIGHT, QUITE a few Americans were talking about the SST and what it was going to do to their ears, and so forth and so on, to those in New York and the East and so forth, when an extremely brilliant vertical threat appeared in the western sky, half blinding all the viewers. At the same moment, the same thing happened to all the eastward viewers in the west. A violet thread, extremely bright.

Meanwhile, the Midwestern viewers were blinded completely for four hours. So much for stargazing!

The ultra-brilliant laser beam penetrated ten miles into the earth, still breaking phonically, sending out ahead of it an extremely great amount of violet light.

The passengers floated lazily up the ten-mile tube and successfully made the White House in Washington, D.C., successfully evading the F. B. I., the C. I. A., and all the other agencies we don't know about.

They stood up to that trembling fool and said, "What the Hell do you think you're doing on this planet?"

CONCERNING TRIBALISM AND LOVING THE WORLD

I CARE VERY MUCH for a few people and let the rest of the world go hang. That's a tribal attitude, isn't it? But at least I've had something to say about the membership of the tribe; or thought I've had something to say, which comes to the same thing.

"If I could save the world—whatever that means—it might be different. But I can't. Oh, I know that the most trivial action of the most insignificant individual might change the world's destiny. But those changes aren't predictable; they're accidents; you can't consciously make them. I'm no Christ or no Napoleon—and neither were they, until they were dead. A person would go crazy if he really thought he could save the world. In any case, the concept of 'world' is an artificial limitation, just like nation or mankind or the solar system or the universe.

"My friends are an extension of my ego, you might say..."

Harworth smiled.

"Can parts of an ego be jealous of each other?" he asked.

"I think so. And if we're not an ego, we're still a kind of organism, or organized pattern. Like a group of adjacent cells, or cells having similar functions."

133

(*Other lines:* that this tribal sympathy is salutary, if only because actual, whereas universal sympathy is abstract—or only a custom, the appearance but not the fact of sympathy. That it provides a basis for advance, since mankind is ripe for it, whereas he is not ripe for love of all mankind. It should not give rise to dangerous, power-seeking cliques, since it seeks and finds pleasure in itself.)

FINAL COMMENTARY

EVERY DAY THE people grew more tired and bored and passively sullen, uninterested and therefore uninteresting.

There was no obvious reason. Peace and plenty reigned. It was the second century of the World Federation. Seventy-five years had elapsed since the War of the Anglo-American Secession, when the English-speaking originators of the Federation had tried to escape from its oppressive equalitarianism. Now the only reminders of that rebellion were certain mildly backward areas on either side of the Atlantic and a tendency on the part of their occupants to reminisce about the Great White Culture and sentimentalize over the vanished beauties of the factory system and the unbalanced wage scale. Even the memories of the Great Civil Wars—northern continents against southern, managers against owners, Asia against the world—were becoming mercifully blurred. Although the last of these, which had wrapped the earth like a shroud and exacted a toll relatively greater than the Black Death, was hardly ten years away.

Technological progress had not been startling. After the astounding spurt of the middle and late Twentieth Century,

135

science had reached a plateau of more gradual ascent. Landscape and climate were well, if indirectly, controlled. Cloud-piercing New Cities rose beside the Old, now become the equivalent of slums. It was largely a wireless, pipeless, roadless world. Atomic power and jet flight were long established. Several of the other planets had been visited by ships.

INSANITY
(2)

WHEN THE INTER-ROOM window remained opaque, Jof Armandy stopped making passes at the control beam and began to pace again, thoughtfully avoiding the black curlicues in the floor design.

If the white-haired girl in the gray form-fitter *had* been Harla, it was easy to understand why she might not want to be seen. When someone who has dropped you ten years ago, with acid recriminations, because you preferred a minor trouble-shooter's post to straight-line administrative careerism, finds out that you've become the pet of the Regional Director, her reactions aren't too difficult to predict.

But what would Harla be doing here? Last he'd heard of her, she'd been power-hunting in the Australasian Region.

And what did Regional Director Stone want with him? Ordinary troubleshooting assignments didn't originate at this office.

His mind reviewed all the recent rumors he'd heard, the new trends he'd sensed, the hunches he'd accumulated, but the answers refused to come.

He switched on the news. A commentator materialized in the center of the room. His ingratiating gaze went over Jof's right shoulder because Jof had avoided the curlicue in front of the control. The commentator's lips curled in a facile smile and he began familiarly, "Say, do you know how it feels to be one of the boys marooned on Ganymede, waiting for the rescue ship? I can tell you, because I just talked over the tight beam with…"

Impatiently, Jof switched on "Summary."

With a flicker the commentator changed pace. His smile faded and, extended finger punching home the emphasis, he telegraphed:

"Three small-regional directors scream for investigation of Director Stone. Try to force meeting of World Council.

"Stone laughs at power-grab story. Brands it X-group rumor.

"Veterans of War of Anglo-American Secession parade over Paris and Rio. Demand super spy system to uncover X-group.

"X-group sabotage hinted in Ganymede Disaster. Rescue ship still three weeks off.

"Psychologist advises passive meditation to cure world-jitters. Dream them away, he says.

"Scholar urges schools to revive instruction in reading. Claims mental discipline will be beneficial.

"Statistics prove we are happier, healthier, wiser, and more mature than ever before. Only X-group stands between individual and absolute personal freedom, says…"

Jof stuck with them for a while, translating the first three into "Those three small-regional directors are probably X-group puppets. Stone's planning a *coup d'etat* against them," and "Stone had the boys parade over Paris and Rio to impress the workers who have refused to go with the slum-city clearance work."

INSANITY /2/

But then his interest flagged. He switched off the projection. The solid-seeming ghost vanished in the midst of his last news-flash.

"He just simply dropped everything, his business and all his affairs and came and nursed Mr. Griswold back to sanity again—did I tell you the poor man nearly went insane with grief? And he's watched over him ever since. Fancy that! It's the most wonderful Christian act I ever saw and even when Mr. Mathia's wife used to come here and beg him to come back to his affairs because you know by this time Mr. Griswold was all right although he never did get over losing his wife, he wouldn't leave him. Said he was afraid he'd collapse again. I don't know what his wife finally did—she didn't like Barstow—too small a place for her—but I think they eventually got a divorce and he's been here ever since looking after poor Mr. Griswold. Isn't it amazing…did you ever hear of anything quite like it…"

Miss Gowrie could see the other man now.

He had his gloved hand on the arm of his companion and his other hand was raised to settle the pince-nez more firmly on his nose.

She could hear his voice too as they stepped down off the kerbstone, the soft slithering sound of it with its unctuous over tones.

"Shall we take a stroll through the park?"

NIGHT RAMBLE

WALKING TOGETHER BY night through the quadrangles, searching for strange buildings to enter silent, for some frightening visitation of the alien. Cold stars and moonlight, eaten at by the glaring pustules of the open street-lights. A mysterious blue luminescence from a window in the chemistry building. Thought of far spaces, terrible distances, other planets. The gargoyles of changeless expression.

Chiefly to make mystery by finding it, or find it by making it. To create adventures half real and half imaginary. A cellar door left open, a fire escape down, the chapel open—these would be excellent raw materials. Who knows what may lurk? This all a shared mood, with neither breaking it by sardonicism.

PRIVACY

CONNIGSBY WAS WALKING the last blocks to work a half hour ahead of most of the other mobile protoplasmic White Collars—as opposed to the more numerous sessile electro-metallic ones—when he saw the Girl shaking the cone-shaped box and talking some gimme-for-a-good-cause patter. She'd hardly be making a sales pitch; street-vending was a misdemeanour in this area even if you had an all-products side and sidewalk license.

Connigsby always went to work a half hour or so early and came home a half hour or more late because he hated tramp-tramping crowds. His wife didn't like defrosting breakfast a half hour early and heat-treating dinner a half hour nearer a civilized seven-thirty. She suspected Connigsby of using the demi-hours for secret drinking or tea-sipping even though he always ate well at both meals and his breath seldom smelled of anything but mouth or at most coke. His co-workers and union liked it even less; to prove he wasn't working overtime for nothing he had to loiter projecting tape-books in the time-clock room, which won him the reputation of being a managerial spy, while the managers suspected him of punching cards, perhaps by short-ranged telekinesis, for late arrivals. But Connigsby willingly, even jestingly bore these small crosses in order to avoid the horror of being one more buggy brigadier in the ant-march.

Connigsby started an illegal slant across the street to dodge the Girl and her patter, although he noted with a twinge of regret that she did indeed have a beautiful slim body, mahogany, not white, outside and presumably continuing on inside her snowy chiton. But what the Hellbomb!—the inward coolth of a meditative morning outweighed the happy annoying zip of briskened-up hormones. There came a chorus of petulant beeps from the droning robotrucks as they radared his human form and corrected course.

Just then Connigsby noticed the word PRIVACY in large red letters around the base of the Girl's collection cone, which looked a little bigger now than he'd first judged it. That word hooked him—he couldn't quite see how it fitted into politics, disease, veterans, or holidays. Who'd be for PRIVACY WEEK except himself and a few other oddballs rolling with an ultra-left or ultra-right torque—the best of both extremes had a lone wolf strain. Besides, his hormones had begun to whine plaintively, just a little. So he slanted back, the robotrucks re-correcting with angry snarls (if you changed your mind three times they reared like lions), and came back to the sidewalk just where the Girl was standing.

She grinned at him, showing pale ivory teeth set in pinkish gums pied with velvet black. Her collection cone seemed smaller again now; it didn't jingle when she shook it.

SEMICENTENNIAL

I SAW THE FIRST moon-shot!"

"Heck, I joined in 1960!"

"I've got a first edition of Clarke's book!"

"I remember Hiroshima!"

"Hoh, hoh! I learned to read on the first issue of *Amazing!*"

"Gentlemen...! Ladies...!" The chairman's magnesium gavel struck the titanium-topped table. Very slowly—to show that they weren't being forced to do it—the group came to order in the low-ceilinged room. They were an interesting lot of oldsters.

THE RED-HEADED
NIGHTMARE

ONCE THERE HAD been numberless golden possibilities, the stars ineffably out of reach had yet beckoned, there had been time to find out and think about it, there had been time and dark room like wombs for hopes and idealisms to grow, there had been room at least in the Western world for adventure and dreams—darkest Africa, darkest Russia, Antarctica, the South Sea Islands, mysterious India, Cathay in its glamorous eternal sunset glow. Room, endless room, like great dark rooms in a house big as the world that a child can explore forever, again and again, with a little candle in his or her hand that shows only a little of them, where he or she can venture again and again, tremulous with fear and delight.

But now, as if some great flashbulb had gone off in space, or rather some great set of cruel Klieg lights had been turned on there and would never again be turned off—these freezing the moment everywhere on Earth, wiping out in an instant all those abovementioned rooms of mystery, showing their darkest secrets in sharp detail, ultimately threatening to wipe out privacy everywhere.

FRITZ LEIBER

And what did this light show? Two great powers—
America and Russian—putting what was superficially the
same question to all the rest of the world: "Slave or Free?"
"Capitalist-exploited or Communist?" (with a salvo of caps).
"Co-operation with *us*, or slavery to *them*?" You can't right it,
you can't run away from it. Once there may have been infinite
golden possibilities, times to dream, room to adventure, but
now there ain't any more, the big flashbulbs have turned on in
space and they'll never turn off again. You got to decide. All
those golden possibilities have narrowed down to one black-
white question—blackest black, white glaring as the flashbulbs glare that even seems to pin your nerves down, show
each secretest cell in your gut and your brain. "Them or us?"
"Slave or free?"

Those two great powers, Russian and America, were chasing all over the world, putting the question to the darkest tribes-
man in the blackest part of the Congo and in Tibet, so often
called the Home of Mystery, the same question was being put, so
there was nowhere to get away from it really. Even space wasn't
the shore of freedom and infinite possibility anymore; Russia
and America had launched a few men out there at vast expense,
billions of dollars and rubles, a percent of one or more of the
national product, a cent or two out of every dollar, a kopeck or
two out of every ruble, so the stars weren't anybody's any more,
to dream about, space belonged to the government, the orbiting
astronauts hid the stars (But which government? America's or
Russia's? Ours or theirs? Slave or Free?).

That light was everywhere, intolerable—even Cathay's
glamorous eternal sunset glow had become...*Red* (*glaringly*
red) China!

Once England and France had put the same question to
the world—Slave or Free?—the Corsican Tyrant's police state

or Britannia ruling the waves (But there had still been the dark places then, the home of mystery, there had been time to think or dream, there was no radio)? And America had been on the side of France then, which had learned revolution from her. They still bowed to the liberty cap atop the pole on the Eastern American Seaboard.

—⁀—

FRED HUMBOLDT'S GRANDFATHER was looked upon as the least reliable member of the family and both his son and grandson were pleased that he was content to live alone, emeritus Professor of Physics at a small Midwestern university in Southern Illinois. He—Friedrich—had *not* fought in WWI, while his son, Gus (which he always preferred to Gustav) *had* fought in WWII— and that was the measure of the difference between the men (Similarly Fred had been christened Fred, not Friedrich or even Frederick). Friedrich had worked in radar during the War (in which his son fought in Germany, there on D-Day and at the Battle of the Bulge), and especially on some of the earliest light-beam communication systems, and he probably would have played a bigger part in the discovery of lasers, but then, a little before it happened to Oppenheim, his security clearance was cancelled because of his association with communist-infiltrated groups during the late '20s and '30s and perhaps because he had signed various ban-the-bomb, etc., petitions. At the time of this security cancelation, his son had broke away, dissociated his family from his father's—through grandmother had rather sided with them—she was a D. A. R., etc.— partly to keep his then about 4-year-old son from possible bad grandparental influence, and it wasn't until the '60s that the families began to see something of another.

A Good thing, that separation, from Gus's point of view, for Fred did have a sneaking well-hidden almost repressed liking for his grandfather, who was soft and imaginative and tolerant where his son (Fred's father) was tough and realistic and unswervingly loyal to the US and its Army and to engineering and the Episcopal Church, etc. Yet Fred inherited the old man's talent and no mistake, he almost went into theoretical physics and optics, but instead into atomics or rather nucleonics and reactors, etc., because that was more practical and because Gus was making it a tradition of two generations that he and his son should be guardians of the bomb and of America. Fred's mother was a good army wife, her chief trouble that she sometimes drank too much—Gus's drinking was perfectly controlled like almost everything else around him, while Friedrich—Grandfather—had been almost a lush. Fred's childhood had been spent on Army posts—Japan, that was during the Korean War; but then the States mostly after that, the Southwest, Chicago (5th Army), but Fred hadn't gone to UofC but been sent out to Cal Tech, first atomics, but then the fields of test-measurement, monitoring, and so into the association with Belz Szeller which had led to his present assignments. He's unmarried—his father Gus's attitude that no women are to be trusted with one's secrets, plus his grandfather's unhappy marriage have convinced him that marriage is not for him—until, at least, his physics-hitch is over and he can marry a young girl and not worry about keeping secrets from her. He's had C. I. A.-type training without ever knowing how far he really was in that organization. He has something of a passion for hand-to-hand combat. He prides himself on his sophistication and control—he's much smoother in these things than his father. He's matured during the Khrushchev period and immediately after. No, he went to Chicago because he couldn't get into Cal Tech or M. I. T., but this didn't bother his father too much now, because Hutchins etc. was out and football is back again (tho Fred's preference is for individual sports on the whole).

His C. I. A.-type training was at a big sort of hunting-lodge school in Penna. It is a rather special and certainly quite secret project to harden up science types—part of training lectures and reading about Communists. Szeller tells him once that this was "play," but clearly is pleased that he had it. At any rate, Fred is trained in this stuff, so he has the proper detection and concealment and communication-back-to headquarters equipment for his work... He's recently been stationed in Geneva with Szeller, though part of the time at Vienna.

THERE WAS PRETTY much a fixed agreement in Fedor Malakov's family never to talk about grandfather Ivan, who had been purged in the 1930s. In fact, there was even a tradition that he had been involved, or taken as involved in the assassination of Kirov. They had always been a Leningrad family. Ivan (the one who went to Siberia and never came back—Vorkuta, at any rate, though they were never sure) had actually been in the Revolution—The Finland Station, the Winter Palace, etc., and he had been a leading minor figure in the Leningrad section of the party during the '20s. There was also the feeling—this very closely hid—that Pavlov Ivanovich had informed on his father—always strained feelings between Grandmother Marienka Marie and her son Pavlov, who is an officer in MVD (previously NKVD, etc.) but Mother Tanya is a good party wife. All three men—Ivan, Pavlov, and Fedor—are or were CP members. Pavlov an engineer, also worked away from Leningrad, but mostly down in the Caucasus. So far Fedor Siberia is associated in his mind with his grandfather; yet he's been there himself, spent those two years in Igarka. He was educated at the Institute of Precision Mechanics and Optics with on-the-job training at Elektrosila. But has had special training for his job with—tho he can't be quite sure— a branch of the KGB. His father still with MVD, although he had a nervous time after the death of Stalin and during the Khrushchev "thaw." Worries because Fedor contributed a poem to second and even more secret handwrit edition of *Yeres*—Heresy.

And now we must go to the spot where these two young men first encounter each other. Now Korovskiy Prospekt, after crossing the Kirov Bridge, dips sharply under the Field of Mars, where there is a heliport and has been built an electric launching tower for daily rocket to Vladivostok, which drops off mail, etc. to various cities en route—near Vorkuta, north end of Baikal, etc. The next launching tower will be at Vladivostok, then one at Moscow. (Leningrad came first because of Elektrosila. Launching tower built in midst despite dangers because of feelings that this spot was never taken in WWII. Something so precious.)

THE UNHUMAN

AT PRECISELY THREE in the afternoon, on schedule as always, the signal came from the bedroom—five tingling sweet bursts of sound, like the striking of a heavenly clock, transfiguring the dingy apartment with its book-and-magazine-weighted shelves that all curved like bows bent downward.

John Wyring straightened up in his easy chair, bumpy with loose springs. The signal had worked an effect on his face too, bringing to it a pride and an adventurous, danger-recognizing alertness rather out of place in a person confined in the monotonous and uncertain Twentieth Century.

At the window, Alice gasped, jerked down the shade, and darted toward the bedroom door. Then John Wyring moved with surprising swiftness for an office worker over forty. He intercepted his wife and threw his arms around her.

"But the unhuman's out there," Alice protested, twisting in his embrace, "the tall one without a left hand, the one that Varden warned us against. I just saw him. We've got to stop Varden, he mustn't come back now."

John Wyring's newly-created poise was shaken barely for a moment by this alarming information. Eyes still fixed on the bedroom door, he unhurtingly tightened his grip on his wife.

"You can't stop Varden," he said softly, but with reassuring confidence. "If you go in the bedroom now, you might obstruct his arrival space, and that would be a lot worse for him, and for you, than his getting the time-bends. You shouldn't have pulled down the shade. The unhuman may have been waiting for that. But Varden will be able to handle things."

By the time he finished, Alice had stopped trying to break away and was clinging to him, as was most natural considering the big things with which they were faced. John Wyring watched the bedroom door over her shoulder, his attitude a lot calmer than his feelings. That an unhuman had turned up now...

TO JONQUIL

NOTHING IS MORE important for me than the wonder and mystery of life, the thrill of a truly new experience. There are a lot of names for the thing I'm after, but most of them are too limited or hedged with errors and conventions, so I discard them—God, "experience," nirvana, peace, inward visions… Wonder and mystery come closer.

You and I are in this quest together, and I imagine you think the same. We are allies. Our equipment consists of minds and bodies—and perhaps social connections. We are, more or less, racked by emotions, prejudices, minor desires, the demands of necessity, social pressures, past commitments. But insofar as any of these things really take command of our actions, we lose sight of the real goal—the never-ending penetration into the realms of the wonderful and the mysterious. Cool-headed wisdom must hold in control the passions that rack us, or see that they are allowed to explode in suitable and limited directions.

One must endure difficulties and delays—and especially learn to "crush joy's grape" against the palate without being overwhelmed by the melancholy that is so apt to follow.

FRITZ LEIBER

If the main quest is to be followed, then there must be an
end to childish impulses—the futile beating against the bars
of necessity, the desire for miracles, the demanding of others
the impossible, the desire to be constantly loved.

LET'S PURSUE HAPPINESS

I.

A PSYCHIATRIST, WHO HAD damn well better remain name-less here, once told me that if a man and wife can't amicably finish a fifth of whisky between them in an evening, there's something wrong with their marital relationship. Of course the psychiatrist had had a few himself. Otherwise he certainly wouldn't have gone on to say that some of his patients were better able to tell their troubles—to pinpoint their emotional difficulties—after a few drinks, if they were drinkers, or after a couple of sticks of marihuana, if they were used to smoking weed.

There's an odd trick of human thought involved here. We feel no moral uneasiness when we hear about a criminal suspect or psychiatric patient being given the "truth drug" scopolamine, because it has a nice long name and calls to mind white coats, hospitals, courts, painless childbirth, and other more-or-less respectable symbols. We applaud its power in "narco-analysis" to draw secrets from the troubled mind. Yet

157

scopolamine is really no different from whisky or weed, it's something to make us warm and woozy, something to blanket the mind and at the same time dissolve its defenses, something to make it easier for us to talk. But weed and whisky have the wrong associations—bars, dens, vice, police. Sensible psychiatrists understand this quirk in human thinking and keep quiet about the cases where hemp or alcohol served as truth serums.

Surgeons find themselves in a similar position. Alcohol is about the best post-operative pain-killer going. But it's given intravenously to spare the tender sensibilities of the patient and his relatives. Of course he misses the reassuring burn at the back of his throat, but his mucus membranes are spared and apparently just having the stuff in his veins is enough to keep him happy while his body starts to heal.

NOTES FOR STUDY OF MAC:
Dec. 29 [1938?]

FIDDLING WITH SMALL object

sensitiveness, easily hurt by small differences in those around him

regard for truth, precise understanding and interpretation of the statements of others.

embarrassed and struck dumb by strangers, particularly those talking argot of their crowd.

a liking for cataloguing and organizing things

an excellent memory; a fairly precise picture of the sequence of his own life (very much more than that of the average intelligent person)

a more active mind; thinks more

well defined likes and dislikes, which are recognized and logically obeyed

All the above is a description of Mac when he is nicely functioning; when not, a general abstraction and sloth intervene; thinking becomes repetitive (?) and dulled; attention wavers; concentration becomes difficult.

PRACTICE WRITING

DO ONE PAGE (or a little more, if so hap) each day. Each piece will be an admitted fragment, and need not have a definite end, or even unity, though it will often naturally tend to have both. It should not take up more than twenty or thirty minutes. These pieces will be in month-cycles. Some cycles will be the writing up of actual experience; others will be imaginative—that is, I will take the facts and indications available and try to work up something that feels plausible.

Here are some cycle-topics: 1) Key moods and experiences of my life; 2) Sketches of people, explanations of them, or imagines bits from their conscious experience; 3) Places as remembered in terms of any or all senses, etc., or imagines; 4) Emotions, such as fear, anger, hate, love, lust, melancholy, irritation, feeling of power, feeling of possession, pain, sense of beauty, sense of being discriminated against, etc. (this would be especially valuable in "breaking the ice," by making me more able to tackle confidently such emotions when they happen to come up in actual writing; even though I have not experienced such emotions to the full in actuality, I will have at least thought through them conscientiously; other emotions or feelings might include fear of death, fear of torture, jealousy, fear of loss of a loved one, emotions while committing murder, while committing theft, etc.); 5) Dialogue—either imagined (between real or imaginary people, or mixed) or real (being a dramatic work-up and essence-rendering of remembered dialogue); 6) Conflicts—this would tend to a still greater degree of unity than the others, which might not be a bad idea at all; it would be like Aeschylus introducing the second actor; and the same would tend to apply to dialogue, though not in all cases by any means; 7) Styles. Here the emphasis would be on form—and on a conscious attempt to vary form daily—rather than on subject matter. Finally, it would not be necessary to adhere absolutely to the cycle-system. If a novelty occurred, it would be well to work it up. But as a general rule, I would follow the cycle faithfully, writing only one type of thing each month.

Here is a tentative schedule for the immediate future:

June and July EMOTIONS AND FEELINGS
August PEOPLE
September PLACES
October STYLES
November MY KEY MOODS AND EXPERIENCES
December DIALOGUE
January CONFLICTS
February EMOTIONS AND FEELINGS

I could work these up while shaving, dressing, etc. perhaps, and then go on to do them very swiftly at the typewriter itself.

THE LUST OF THE ALIEN

BUT IT IS a guilty secret that we share," said F., smiling earnestly into the darkness. "This lust for the alien, this breathless interest in the bizarre. Think how other people would shake, shake their heads and laugh pityingly—but kindly, too; and I mean those people who are intellectually akin to us, the ones we go to class with and talk with. You know."

The spot of darkness which was M. sent forth its abstract quivering voice. "Toyah, yes. There's another thing. They'd be very apt to mistake it. They might confuse it with the typically adolescent interest in perversions, psychological and criminal and so forth; excursions into Kraft-Ebbing and Huysmans, pretences at being able to appreciate the mentality of a Crippen or Giles de Retz. Background music for a sophisticated withdrawal—which makes its exit when normal sexuality is developed."

"Or they might even—I really don't think I go too far— connect it up with spiritualism and so with religion in general and so with Christianity in particular. And even if they saw through those misconceptions, their final judgement would possibly only come to: rebellion against science and reality."

"I believe in the Elder Gods because I cannot adjust myself to a class-conscious society?" intoned the darkness.

"Something like that. At all events, they'd only see the negative side of it—what is *isn't* rather than what it is. They'd miss the inner thrill, the spell of darkness, and vast distances, and dimension piled on dimension, and boundless alien possibilities hemming us round and threatening."

"Ah, yes,"—the voice seemed to disengage itself from possible metaphysical speculation.

"When, really, we're in closer league with science than they suspect."

"It occurs to me that certain chords of music might be capable of sending people into a paroxysm of terror."

"Given the right atmosphere; given the right build-up; given the right people."

"No! Given nothing except the music. Can't you see it? The lights begin to dim—as they always do. The audience settles itself, murmuring. A perfectly commonplace-looking man walks slowly to the piano; no Boris Karloff-Bela Lugosi stuff, no black gloves and sunken eyes. Nothing like that. He makes a quick, unimpressive bow. The scattered applause dies away. He seats himself and, using little force, strikes a complex chord. Then another. Not loud. A sound like a quick hiccupy sigh comes from the audience. They strain in their seats in subtly peculiar angles—like people who have died while straining to free themselves from thin cords with which they have been tied. Then another chord, a little louder. That sets them loose. They stampede. They trample over each other. Some leap from the back of one seat to another, treading heads and shoulders. Most of these go down, clawing. Others crawl under the seats, not mindful of the trampling, perhaps welcoming it. But the only sound is that made by their scrambling. There is hardly any tramp of feet—they are pressed together too closely for that. And—here's the important point—there are no screams, no cries of any sort; their vocal mechanisms have immediately gone into a state of psychic-anaesthesis. Who knows why? Perhaps they fear that any sound they might make would be the same as that coming from the accursed piano."

"That sounds a little pat. Are you telling a story?"

"Of course. And it won't seem pat when you hear the final touch. They do make certain noises—windy grunts *pressed* out of them by the squeezing and elbowing and kicking of the mob. Meanwhile the pianist begins a series of arpeggios, breaking up the original chords, turning them into runs, sucking out even more of the ultimate horror."

"Ah, ha, that's where your tale falls apart. You remember, you insisted this music didn't depend on the people or the build-up. Then why is the pianist immune from the general terror."

M.'s face lit up. He grinned like a whimsical satyr.

"The pianist is stone-deaf," he said.

L. laughed snorting, obviously, but heartily.

"A hit, a hit; a very palpable hit."

"Well, again," F. continued good-naturedly. "There are only a limited number of notes on a piano or any other instrument, you must admit. Why, then, isn't it that these chords haven't been struck by accident?"

"Ah," said M. "But it isn't an ordinary piano—no, nor even an ordinary half-tone piano."

IN THE
BEGINNING

IN THE BEGINNING
An Introduction by Fritz Leiber

THE TRUE BEGETTER of this little book of two science instructive stories and four historical moral tales for Christian children was the Reverend Ernest W. Mandeville, whom back in the 1930s we called "Beezie." He was stalwart and prematurely bald like Little Orphan Annie's mysterious benefactor Daddy Warbucks.

The comparison is apt, for Beezie was another self-willed, venturesome, energetic precedent-bending hero of Depression times. And he was theater-struck—that was what attracted him to my Shakespearean father and mother. He was the Episcopalian priest in Middletown, New Jersey, and they had a summer place in nearby Atlantic Highlands.

When I first met Beezie in the summer of 1932, he also ran an advertising agency in New York City, supervised an employment bureau for Episcopal clergymen there, and edited the religious journal, *The Churchman*. There were other things he was into, but I forget them. While I'd just got my bachelor's degree from the University of Chicago and won a graduate scholarship, but hadn't the faintest idea of what I wanted to do with it or with myself.

The result of this encounter of strong and wavering wills seems inevitable to me now, though it shocked my University friends then. Beezie persuaded me to spend the next academic season running two missionary Episcopal churches under his loose supervision in Atlantic Highlands and nearby Highlands, while weekdays attending in residence the General Theological Seminary in downtown Manhattan, board and tuition free.

I was successful in my new and very unfamiliar work conducting services that didn't require a priest, preaching short sermons, and building up church attendance, while at the Seminary I got good grades and enlarged my knowledge, but bowed out uncomfortably at the end of the year, having decided I didn't have a real call to be a preacher, spent the next season back at Chicago floundering around on a reduced scholarship, by which time I'd discovered that I wanted, at least tentatively, to be a writer.

With admirable lack of resentment for my failing him and also great practicality, Beezie when he heard of this suggested I begin by writing children's stories for *The Churchman* at $15 or $20 per, I think it was, a good price then.

So during the summer of 1934, when my father was preparing what turned out to be his last Shakespearean tour, and where I'd act with him, I began grinding out the little stories in this book, writing the last of them in some lonely western hotel room while on tour and trying to make all of them fit their market. This writing work emboldened me to start, on various hotel stationeries, an adventure novel about a lost Mayan civilization. That project fizzled out after some thirty pages, but the six children's stories got done and appeared in *The Churchman* between Oct. 1, 1934, and April 15, 1935.

In The Beginning: *An Introduction*

My father made his contribution to my new avocation (it took me twenty more years to become a full-time writer) by having me write the stories of *King Lear, Macbeth, Hamlet, The Merchant of Venice,* and *Julius Caesar,* the five plays we did, for our deluxe program book, not quite as good practice for a fledgling author as writing new stories, but very helpful.

Looking through the six children's tales now, I'm mostly struck by the gaps in my knowledge, which were not always corrected by sufficient story-research. My worst subject was history. I'd been put off it by the repeated patriotic American history courses I'd been put through in grammar and high school, boring and unreal. At the seminary I'd had good courses in Old Testament and early church history, but those were all.

So in "Children of Jerusalem" I have that city importing apples as rare delicacies from across the Mediterranean and camel-trucking pomegranates through the desert from Babylon, which is pretty funny if you consider Eve's apple and Solomon's pomegranates. (This weakness on fruits stuck with me a long while. In my authorized ghosting of *Tarzan and the Valley of Gold* in 1966 I have lost-civilization Incans growing pineapple *trees.* Well, I guess I thought that since the pine and apple were both trees, how could their combination be anything less?) And I write about the king and queen of Israel as if it were England.

While the Professor in the balloon stories doesn't seem to have heard of the innumerable galaxies of stars dotting near-infinity beyond the stars of our own Milky Way. Maybe he or I thought that would make it too complicated for the children, which would have been insufferably patronizing of us. Or maybe I didn't know too well myself. Astronomy was another science, like botany, I was weak on then—no courses in either.

FRITZ LEIBER

I'm struck at the stuffy Professor adding to his pious "God is everywhere" the rider "He is where all good things are"— and not where all evil things are, also? Was I a Manichean heretic when I wrote that, or just trying to depersonalize God into the Good?

At least the old Prof propagandizes the kids on the possibility of there being other intelligent beings in the universe besides man. He's got that going for him.

And I'm touched by little Amos in the two Jesus stories, where at least I had the good sense not to bring Christ on stage. The lonely street-boy wise to crowd behavior, curious about everything but hesitant to commit himself to anything, is more of a character than the other kids. With him I begin to bring myself into the stories, both as I was and as I would have liked to have been.

Though I doubt John the Baptist would have been so approvingly tolerant of his hesitation to join up. But I have no excuses for misspelling "lizard" with two z's. "Buzzard" is the only like word I can think of that takes two z's—which is something I remember now by thinking of an old man on trial for witchcraft in Salem in 1692 expostulating to his judges, "You tax me for a wizard. You might as well tax me for a buzzard!" Strange are the ways of mnemonics.

My spelling got past the *Churchman* editors, but here it has been corrected.

Fritz Leiber
October, 1982

THE ADVENTURES
OF THE BALLOON

TOM AND ELSIE had bought a toy balloon filled with gas. They were taking turns holding it so that it wouldn't get away. As they were walking past the Professor's house they noticed him looking up at the different clouds in the sky. He was an elderly man with a little gray beard and a pleasant face; he taught at the university. He waved at the children and they came in to see him.

After he had given them two cookies apiece, Elsie said, "Professor, we want to know what would happen if we let this balloon go up into the air. Tom says it would go on up forever, but I think it would hit the sky and stop—the way it does when it hits the ceiling of a room." "Well," answered the Professor, "let's all suppose you and Tom were so small that you could get into a match box, tie it to the balloon and go up with it. At first you would be jounced around and blown in different directions, for the winds are piled up on top of each other and some go one way and some another."

"Would we be so small that we'd have to dodge the clouds?" asked Elsie.

"No, you'd go right through them, for they're just a fog that's high up. But you'd be pretty cold and damp until you got into the sunlight above them. By that time the little balloon would have taken you as high as it could go. You'd have to let out some gas and come down slowly or else it might explode and then you'd come down *kerplunk!*"

"Only, if we were that small," said Tom, "we'd have parachutes made out of pocket handkerchiefs and get down safely."

"But suppose," Elsie insisted, "we had a much, much better balloon. What would happen then?"

"You'd go on up and up, up above the highest clouds, which are made of tiny ice-needles. The air would get so thin that you have to take along tanks of it to breathe."

"Just like a submarine takes when it goes down under the water," said Tom. "And then would you keep on going up and up forever?"

"No," answered the Professor. "The balloon only goes up because it is lighter than the air around it. Now the air only goes up so far. When the air gives out, the balloon can't go up any further and begins to come down."

"But if it *could* go up further, it would bump the sky, wouldn't it?" asked Elsie.

"No, if it could go up that way it would keep on going until it got as far as the stars and then even go beyond them."

"Gee," said Tom, "that's a long way. What is beyond the stars, anyway?"

"I don't know," answered the Professor. "The telescopes can't see that far."

"Maybe God lives on the other side of the stars," said Elsie.

"God created the stars, just like He made the world and you and me," said the Professor. "And whatever there may be on the other side of the stars, He made it. But God Himself is everywhere. He is where all good things are."

"Professor," said Tom, after a pause, "is there any way of getting up higher than a balloon can go?" "Well, no one has done it, but you might be able to do it in a sky-rocket, though it would have to be a much bigger one than those you see on the Fourth of July." "Boy, you'd go up faster even than an aeroplane then," said Tom, and his eyes sparkled.

"Is there anything that lives up above the clouds?" said Elsie. "I mean outside of the birds that fly that high." "Well, there might be some Hyups," said the Professor.

"Who are the Hyups?" asked Elsie.

"Well, I'm not sure there are any Hyups," said the Professor. "But there *might* be. Would you like to hear a Maybe Story about them?"

"Oh yes," said Tom and Elsie in one voice.

"Once upon a time they lived on the earth," said the Professor. "They were little animals like kangaroos, but they could jump even higher than kangaroos because they had lungs that were very large and were filled with the same kind of gas that a balloon is filled with. They even looked a bit like balloons that had sprouted arms and legs and heads. And they weren't called Hyups then, but Bouncers; they lived up north where it's very cold. Then one year they decided to come south and so all of them set out hopping along merrily. But the first hot day the gas inside of their lungs expanded and they went sailing up into the air. When they got up on top of the clouds the sun shone even more warmly and there didn't seem to be any chance of getting down, unless they could grab onto a stray falling star, which was unlikely. Moreover, they liked it pretty well up there as they were far away from their enemy, the Sword-beaked Lizard, who used to make their lives miserable by puncturing their gasbags. They even began to call themselves Hyups, because they were high up. So they took to living on top of the clouds, nourished by mist and sunshine. All they ever see is an occasional bird and the only thing they fear is a pinprick. There are a great many of them living up there and the clouds are their kingdom."

"My geography teacher never told me about the Hyups," said Elsie.

"She couldn't very well," laughed the Professor, "for no one knows whether there really are any Hyups. Nevertheless, there *might* be. I guess we'll have to call them Maybe People. And don't you children ever tell Professor Brown what I said about the Hyups. He would insist that I prove that there are such things and I can't do that because I don't know."

By this time Tom and Elsie saw that it was time to go. As they went Tom called back, "If Elsie and I get small and this balloon carries us away, we'll be sure to let you know if we see any Hyups."

AFTER the DARKNESS

SILENT AS THE others, little Amos sat in the shadow of the rough table, his back against the dried clay wall. He felt very sad and the darkness did not disturb him, though it did not comfort him either. The little oil lamp flickered without defiance against the black night pressing in through the small, high windows. Of what use was its light to gruff, kindly Peter, who had sat without moving or speaking since he'd come in hours before? It only let one see the despair and guilt in his narrowed eyes, the horror in John's wide, handsome eyes. Let John see without respite the few other disciples, none with good news to tell. The little lamp could hardly fight against the dark smoke of its dying wick. It only irritated the men in the little clay house. It brought no hope. The Master was dead.

Amos was tired as well as sad. The last few days had been very full, since Peter and John had found him in the streets of Jerusalem tired and hungry, without home or family, chased by unfriendly gangs of boys, ignored by the crowds, suspected by shopkeepers when he came asking for errands to run. But Peter and John had befriended him, given him a home to live in and chores to do. In those days he had met the Master, learned to worship and to love Him—to learn that did not take long. During those days he had come to see how a boy could really look forward to becoming a man.

But now that was all over. The Master was dead.

First there had been the excitement and triumph of the Master's entry into Jerusalem. Then suspicion and betrayal. The trial. The mob before Pilate—the most terrible one Amos had ever seen, and Amos had seen many mobs. Then Golgotha and the Master's death; the end of His teaching; the end of His love; the end of hope.

Crouching among the silent men in the little clay room, Amos felt once again homeless. It was like the night he had stood in the chilly street and realized for the first time that there was not one door in the city that would admit him if he knocked. He felt out of place, as though he were intruding upon the disciples in their great grief. Now that the Master was gone he had no chance in life.

The little lamp had almost flickered out. Everywhere was painful silence. He closed his tired eyes and slept.

For a time he knew nothing.

Then into the darkness of his dreaming came a voice that said over and over again only one word—"Alive!" Amos blinked and half-opened his eyes. Sunlight flooded the room. A wildly excited woman was telling something to the disciples that held them breathless. Amos raised his head over the edge of the table and gulped in her words.

The Master was alive! He had been dead and now was alive again. He had spoken to them; His words had been words of joy.

Amos quickly looked back and forth from the face of Peter to the face of John. Their joy was his joy; he felt it way down in his heart. That deep joy was there for good; whatever might happen to him, that could not be taken away. Never again would he know the complete despair of the past night. The Master had conquered death.

Amos walked down toward the door. Peter had just dashed through it and run down the street, his footsteps drumming merrily on the morning air. On the table Amos noticed the little lamp; dry and empty save for the charred wick. He stood in the door, breathing the sleepiness and sorrow out of his body and the clear air in. His eyes were filled with the glory of the risen sun.

CHILDREN OF JERUSALEM

MANY CENTURIES BEFORE Jesus came to Jerusalem, Naomi and her brother Nahum lived there in a crowded part of the city in a house built of clay bricks. Their father was a well-to-do fruit merchant; he even owned a tiny, walled garden that adjoined the house.

On one hot summer day the two children played that they were king and queen of the country and pretended that the other children were their subjects. There was a stone bench in the garden that they called their throne. Nahum sent his soldiers out to conquer the people of other countries; Naomi sent all the children she did not like into exile or had their heads chopped off. Of course, they didn't tell the other children what they were doing as they were afraid of some of the bigger ones. Besides, as Naomi said to her brother, it was just make-believe and wouldn't hurt anyone.

When Zachariah, their father, came home from the market he was in a good humor. After supper he gave them each a pomegranate and, as they sucked the juice from each ruby seed, he told them what had happened that day.

"Those pomegranates came in on a great caravan from the western countries around great Babylon; they were wrapped in large leaves to shield them from the heat of the desert sun. Ships from the north brought a fruit that they say the sailors call apples. I bought many of them; the rich are always wanting something new to taste."

"Did anything else happen in the market, daddy?" asked Nahum.

"Oh yes, something exciting is always going on. Soldiers marched past bringing debtors from the outlying farmlands. It is rumored that our king plans to make war on Moab. A nobleman drove his chariot past at such a reckless speed that he almost hit Elias the Jeweler. And in the afternoon another prophet came in from the desert. He jumped on top of some bales of cloth newly arrived from Egypt and shouted that we merchants were robbers and cheats and unpleasing to Jehovah because of our sharp dealings. He was laughed at for a time and then some of the younger men chased him away. Of course he was foolish to be impolite, but there is much truth in what he said. We are all looking out for ourselves and try-ing to make money and have no time to think of those who are poor and unlucky. But business is business and it is hard to see a remedy."

"Did the strange man look very fierce?" questioned Nahum excitedly.

"He was thin and sunburned and looked wild, lean, and hungry. But don't get too excited about him; there is always a new prophet coming to Jerusalem."

When they woke up the next morning Naomi told her brother that she had dreamt that the prophet was a wild look-ing man who carried a great knife. So, when they went out into the garden, Nahum pretended he was the prophet and jumped up on the stone bench and shouted and chased Naomi with a wooden sword. Then Naomi would play she was a soldier and catch the prophet and after that she would play she was the queen and sentence him to death. It made a very exciting game.

When they were playing it for the third time in spite of the fact that it was a very hot day, Nahum opened the door leading to the street and started to run out to avoid being captured. But, going through, he stumbled over the body of a man lying there. He had a white beard and looked as though he had been starved and beaten. He was unconscious.

"He must have fainted from the heat," said Naomi. "Let's see if we can help him."

So they half carried him, for he weighed very little, to the stone bench under the trees that they called the king's throne. Nahum brought water and bathed his face and wrists, while Naomi got salve and put it upon his bruises. Then he began to breathe more easily and finally he opened his eyes and looked at them slowly. They were silent, for the great brown eyes commanded their attention.

Then he said, "You have helped me, and I thank you for it. In return I will tell you something. You are the children, and the children shall rule Jerusalem; you will be the soldiers and the merchants, the priests and the shopkeepers, even the king and queen."

"We have a game and in it we play that we are king and queen," said Naomi. Then she held out a small bowl. "You must be very thirsty," she said.

The old man drank the water, then turned to them and asked, "How do you play this game?"

"It's a lot of fun," said Nahum. "We send out our soldiers to fight the armies of our enemies and capture their cities. This morning we caught a bad prophet and put him to death."

"Yet you were kind to me when I fell down exhausted at your door. Why do you pretend to do such mean things when you are king and queen?"

"But kings and queens always do things like that," said Nahum. "They have to."

"No," said the old man, "kings and queens can do what they please. The rulers and leaders in a land can be cruel or kind. They decide what is to be done and therefore they have the power to work for war or for peace. The same is true of any man or woman. Let me tell you a new way to play your game. Think of all the good things that you might do in Jerusalem if you were king and queen. Find ways to help the poor people and to make peace with other nations."

"That would be a fine game," said Naomi. "We ought to have thought of it before."

"I will leave you to play it," said the old man. "I feel better now and must be on my way."

He took with him a little fruit that they gave him. As he walked out of the garden door he turned and said, "Remember, the children shall rule Jerusalem." Then he was gone. Nahum and Naomi immediately began to play that they were building houses for the poor people that had no place to live.

Just then their father ran into the garden, very much excited. "Are you children all right?" he said. "I just saw that prophet, that wild man I told you about, going out of the garden gate."

"Was *that* the prophet?" said Nahum. "Why, he was a gracious and kind old man. He was tired, and we gave him something to eat and drink."

"And before he left, he told us something," Naomi went on. "He said that the children would rule Jerusalem. Now, no one would let us do that. What do you think he meant by it?"

Their father thought for a moment and said, "Those who *will* be kings and leaders in this country are now only children. Some day the fate of Jerusalem and of the whole world will be in the hands of those who today are young and have no responsibilities. Some day you will take over my business, Nahum, and will have to see to it that the customers and the other traders are treated fairly. You, Naomi, will have your duties too. Perhaps that was what he meant."

"Perhaps," said the children, and they began to play a game in which they avoided war with the Philistines by seeing to it that their subjects were very careful not to offend or injure people from other countries.

FURTHER ADVENTURES
OF THE BALLOON

I'M WARNING YOU now, children," said Professor Brown, approaching along one of the garden paths. "You won't find any fish in that pool."

"We're not fishing," Elsie called to him and then turned back to watch Tom.

The professor came up to the edge of the pool. It was a rather deep one. Tom seemed to be poking at the bottom with a long stick.

"Did you lose something in the water?" asked the professor.

"No," said Tom, keeping a careful hold on the pole. "We're conducting a scientific experiment."

"Well, that's rather in my line, Tom. Are you looking for sea-serpents?"

"No, it's something even more scientific than that," muttered Tom darkly and gave the professor a mysterious look.

"Do try it now, Tom," Elsie cut in. "I'm tired of waiting."

"All right, but remember to watch carefully," Tom replied and let go of the pole. There was an unexpected splash; a red globe popped out of the water, jumped up a few inches into the air, and then dropped back to the surface, where it floated gaily.

"Isn't that the toy balloon you showed me yesterday?" said the professor. "You children certainly take good care of it. That was a fine experiment."

Tom looked up at him delightedly. "We tied a stick to it so that we could pull it down to the bottom. And we took some of the air out first so that it wouldn't break going down."

"And what did you discover by making this experiment?"

"We found out that it was hard to pull it down under the water and we found out that it came up so fast that it jumped right out of the water," Elsie answered quickly. The professor nodded.

"Mr. Brown," said Tom, "what would happen if we made it go down much deeper than that— If we made it go down to the bottom of the ocean?"

"Well, we'd have to find some way of getting it down that wouldn't strain the rubber too much. Then, as it went down, the water on top of it would press on it more and more—compress it; it would get tinier and tinier." "Then if I made a big rubber bag could I go down deep into the sea inside it?" questioned Tom excitedly. "No, because you couldn't stand the pressure of the compressed air any more than the pressure of the sea water alone. But you could build a strong hollow ball of steel and go down inside of that."

"Would there be windows to look out of?" asked Elsie.

"Yes," said the professor. "Very, very thick ones." "Then what would we see if we went down for miles and miles?"

"No one has ever gone down much more than half a mile in such a sphere, but we'll suppose we have a stronger one with cables attached to raise and lower it. As we go down we'll turn off the lights inside our sphere so that we can see what is outside. For the first few yards there is still some sunlight coming down through the water. But it gets darker and darker.

We have to turn on our searchlight. We may find that some of the strange fish give off a light of their own, like fireflies. And finally, when we land on the bottom just like a balloon lands on the earth, we might meet the Deep Ones."

"Who are they?" asked Tom.

"Oh, some of the Maybe People that live at the bottom of the sea. They don't even notice the tremendous water-pressure, as they are built to stand it. They think that the water above them is the sky. And when an occasional ship sinks down to them from the top of the sea, they puzzle over it just as we puzzle over the meteors, the 'shooting stars,' that fall down out of our sky."

"But there really aren't any such people, Mr. Brown?" questioned Elsie.

"I don't know. There may be. There may be all sorts of strange people of whom we know practically nothing, of whom we know only that they are cared for by God. All peoples, however different, are united by God.

"But look, children, your balloon has floated way out of reach. How will you get it?"

"I know," said Tom. "We'll throw stones beyond it and then the little waves will wash it ashore."

RICHES AND POWER

NAHUM AND NAOMI stepped up into a doorway to get out of the way of the dust that was swirling up from the pavement. Their faces were eagerly turned back to watch the long line of slaves who were carrying goods through the high-walled street of ancient Jerusalem. They noted the shape of the various bundles and tried to guess their contents.

"That soft, sagging one may have expensive cloth inside it," said the girl, "perhaps pretty dresses."

"I'll bet that little box contains rich spices," answered her brother. "I do believe I can smell them from here. And just see that iron-bound chest—the one that the guard is walking beside. It likely holds money or jewels." Naomi laughed. "Perhaps all the money inside has been spent and the owner is just having it carried around to show off. But look! What is that great, round covered thing? Nahum, I think there are song birds in it. Listen, you can hear them singing!"

A thin-legged boy crowded into the doorway with them. Nahum pushed him over to one side. "Get out of the way, David," he said. "Can't you see that we're watching the slaves go past?"

David rubbed his elbow where it had bumped against the wall. "My, but you're strong, Nahum," he replied, and turned to watch the procession with an intentness that puzzled the children.

A few moments later, as they were going home, a chariot came bumping down the street and drew up beside the line of toiling slaves. A richly dressed, distinguished looking man began to give instructions to one of the overseers.

"When I grow up," said Nahum, "I shall be well-to-do like he is and have servants and slaves of my own. Perhaps David will be one of them; he's only the son of a poor workman and won't be able to get on in the world." "Just the same, you shouldn't be so rough with him," Naomi interrupted, "though I'm sure I'd like to be a great lady and have servants to wait on me."

After supper, while they were sitting out in the garden under the brilliant stars, listening to the exciting night noises of the city, Nahum said, "When I grow up I shall do many great things. I shall be a richer man even than my father."

Naomi did not answer, but she thought to herself, "I believe Nahum is afraid of being thought a poor man or a coward; he talks so much about being rich and strong."

The next morning the garden was bright with sunshine. The children saw David and a couple of other children standing outside the gate and called them in to play.

"I have a new game," said Nahum. "I will be a rich man and you will all be my servants. We'll pretend that these toys are my property and treasure and you will carry them to another city—I mean to the other side of the garden."

"Fine," said David, picked them all up in his arms and was half-way there before Nahum could call out, "You can't go that fast from one city to another; you'll get all tired out. And one servant can't carry all those goods. There's enough there for a hundred men."

"But I can do it easily," responded David.

"No, you can't," shouted Nahum. "Anyway, in this game you have to pretend that you can't. Come back and we'll begin all over again. We'll make a camp half-way across to stay in when it's night."

So they played the game for a while. Then, in the midst of one of their most exciting trips when they were pretending that their caravan was attacked by robbers, they heard the sound of a real procession.

David looked up eagerly. "Those are the men you saw yesterday—the servants of Eleazar the rich landowner. They are returning with more goods. My father is among them. I'm going out and wave to him."

Soon all the children were crowded tightly against a wall on one side of the street, watching the servants, the mules, and the wagons go by. As one of the latter was approaching, David began to wave to a man even thinner than himself who was carrying a bundle. "That's my father," he said.

When the man saw David he smiled, stopped, and straightened up to wave at him. His hand brushed the mule close behind him. The animal shied off to one side, jolting a couple of packages out of the cart. The burly driver jumped ahead angrily, shouted "You stupid slave" at David's father and brought the whip down upon his body. But, as he brought it back to strike again, David leaped in and grabbed the end of the whip. The children were amazed; so was the driver. He tried to jerk the whip out of the boy's hands but, although he pulled this way and that, David would not let go. The man had just let go and was advancing menacingly when there came an interruption. The chariot they had seen the day before clattered down the street and came to a stop. A single commanding word from the tall man in it and all in the street stood stock-still.

"It is Eleazar the Rich," they murmured.

The one inside stepped out and began to determine, by quiet questioning, the cause of the dispute. The mule driver was voluble in his answers; David's father hardly spoke at all; David himself was honest and clear in his answers.

Finally the tall questioner raised his hand. "I have heard enough," he said. "You, driver, are far in the wrong. The man whom you struck, moreover, is overworked; we will see to it that he is rested and restored to health. David, you are a courageous boy and not afraid to stand up for what you think is right. Come to my house tomorrow and I will see to it that you are taught a good trade. And now—take up your loads and go on."

The crowd that had gathered murmured in relief and approval. "I should have done what David did," Nahum said, as he and his sister pushed their way nearer. "Wasn't the rich man powerful and brave."

Eleazar heard this remark and turned back toward them. "Children," he said, in a musing, kindly voice, "I see that you are dazzled by my wealth. But remember—even a rich man is only powerful when he does good and only brave when God gives him the strength to do good. In those ways you can all be more brave and powerful than I."

THE ROAD TO JORDAN

AMOS WAS SITTING in a doorway, waiting for something to happen, when he noticed a small crowd of people making their way through the outskirts of Jerusalem. Because it was not an ordinary crowd he decided to follow it and investigate.

Amos was small, quick, and wiry and often had a dirty face. He lived alone with his mother in a tiny room in a large tenement, except for the times when they had no work and no money to rent even a tiny room. Then Amos lived in the streets, sleeping and eating when and where he could. When his mother had a job she worked very hard all day; he was sometimes able to help her by running errands for merchants or delivering packages for shopkeepers. Whatever Amos did was in the streets of Jerusalem. He seldom saw the insides of houses or other buildings. The streets were his life. Because he was used to them, their crowds did not excite him. But because he was sharp-eyed and independent he was immensely interested in crowds and, in his way, even studied them. He was a sort of expert on crowds.

He watched the people who went to work and the people who went to play and the people who walked the streets because they had nothing to do, work or play. He watched the traders bring food and clothing into the city and watched the merchants sell them. He watched the soldiers; he could tell when they were going off to war and when they were on leave and when they were on police duty and when they were going in a body to make a complaint because their wages had not been paid. Many were the things that he learned from the sound of footsteps and the tone of chattering voices. He could tell a crowd of Pharisees from a crowd of Sadducees without even bothering to look.

So Amos could say to himself with some authority that this crowd was unusual. As it walked through the overcast dawn it might have been a group going to attend a service at a synagogue, only there were no services at that hour and, besides, they looked too aroused. Of course, Amos might have asked one of them where they were going (some of them were children like himself), but he felt that would have been an unfair way of getting an answer; here was a problem, and he wanted to solve it all by himself.

There were about forty people and for the most part silent, though they looked excited enough to chatter for hours. Amos walked along with them without making himself conspicuous. They made their way toward the edge of the city and suddenly turned down a cross street. "This is the way toward the gate," thought Amos. "What can these city folks be wanting in the country? They have no bundles with them, so they can't be moving or going on a long visit."

The sun had now come out and was well up in the sky; down the dusty road marched the little band. Amos hesitated a moment and then set out after them. He knew the country-side quite well and was determined to find out what this new thing was that was happening in it. So on he went, sometimes trudging with them along the road, sometimes making little excursions into the cooler fields, but always keeping up.

After a while they came to a place where a small path branched off. Amos recognized it and walked up to a tall man who seemed to be the leader of the band.

"The road ahead is very bad and long," he said. "The side road is a shortcut."

Some of the people were suspicious of his advice at first. They thought he might be trying to play a joke on them. But they saw a peasant and one of them asked him which was the shortest way to the river Jordan; he pointed to the side road. They thanked Amos, the tall man giving him a curious look, and set out.

Soon the air became cooler; they passed over a small rise and saw the Jordan, a slow-running river, rocks about it, the desert beyond. The little road that they were following ended at the river; there was nothing in sight, house or person. They stood there silently for a moment; then the tall man walked ahead a few paces and called out, "John! John the baptiser!"

There was no answer. He called again,

"Come forth, John. See, we have come unto you that our sins may be washed away. Come forth, John!" Again they waited. Then, without speaking, one of the women pointed down the river; their eyes followed her hand. From behind some high rocks was coming a man, walking with easy assurance and with head held high, although he was dressed only in skins—more poorly than a beggar, thought Amos. Slowly the crowd moved down to meet him; only Amos stayed behind, which was curious, as Amos was usually inquisitive; however, he watched.

What happened did not take long. The man called John greeted them, not loudly, but apparently with kindness; then, one after another, he baptised them simply in the water of the river. He talked to them all for a little time. Then the crowd turned back toward Jerusalem, their faces full of light. John sat down upon a rock by the river; Amos still waited at the top of the hill, watching and thinking. The low talk of the crowd died away. The two were left alone.

After a while Amos saw John turn his head and felt his eyes upon him, the wild eyes he remembered hearing about, the eyes of John the baptiser; he was afraid. But John called out to him in an easy voice,

"Hello, little boy; come down and see me."

So, overcoming his fear, Amos made his way down.

"Sit down—on one of these rocks; there's nothing better," said John in a kindly voice. "Did you come with that crowd?"

"No, sir," answered Amos, "I was just following them along to see what it was like."

"Hmf," muttered John. "And you didn't come down to be baptized—just to see what it was like?"

"Oh, no," said Amos, "I couldn't do anything like that unless I felt I was ready for it."

John looked at him queerly. "Well, that shows you're honest, at least. Mighty few of the people that come out here have any doubts as to whether *they're* ready to be baptised. And most of them begin to forget before they get back to Jerusalem that it was in *hope* of forgiveness of sins that they were baptised."

Amos looked at the ill-dressed man for a moment and then said, "I want to be baptised some day."

John looked back at him and smiled.

It was getting late in the afternoon. Amos was on the road back to Jerusalem. As he walked into the evening the face of John was in his memory, a lean, sun-browned face, a wild, almost wolf like face, but a face that smiled.

POETRY
BY
FRITZ LEIBER

THE DEMONS
OF THE UPPER AIR

I.

There is a whispering outside the walls,
A thing upon the roof,
Come from the shadows, most like a shadow,
But a shadow with teeth and hooking claws,
A whispering shadow.
The hearts that hug the fire within
Beat faster, move closer,
Snuggle down in their pocket of safety,
Opposing the threat from the alien reaches,
Holding their ears against the voice
Of the thing from the thin, high air.
It whispers of conflicts behind the low clouds,
Of creatures nearer and creatures stranger
Than those in the shielding house would wish;
In penetrant treble it whispering sings
The challenging song of those who ride
Where the air thins out to emptiness;

And its voice goes low again to tell
Of the terrible insecurity
Of the whirling, plunging earth.
Let the dwellers within shut their ears,
Stuff cranny and crack, bolt shutter and door and
    inner door—
There still comes a murmuring down past the fire,
Against the smoke and the pushing heat,
Tainting even the roaring of the fire:
A whispering outside the walls,
A thing upon the roof.

II.

Solomon sought to seal us up,
Thinking we were a book a man might seal,
Thinking we were strange pictures
And our racing thoughts
But dimming words upon a yellowed page.
Lo, Solomon is dead
And we still ride the upper air
Above a newer Babylon.
Upon the cold moon's spaceward side
Our fortress stands, the gates rust not;
Out on the last, unknown sphere
That rings the sun our pennon flies;
And men still hear above their heads
Our whistling cries, our trumpet calls,
And see, gigantic, menacing,
Our shadows on their tallest walls.
True, true indeed, a book are we,

The Demons of the Upper Air

A book that was penned by the elder gods,
A book that never a man may seal.

III.

Above, above
The air is thin, the sky is bright;
Come up, soft sister, through the night.
Around, around
The far stars wheel, the space winds surge
Against the dwellers on the verge;
The sky is black, the sky is bright;
Leave dreaming to the lower night.
Leave, leave
Your body to the earth,
Small sins to hell, small plans to mirth;
Cast, cast away
All lesser fear
To cumber still the cumbered sphere;
Slip, slip
Your silky, soft cocoon
And rise through madness to our noon.
Your soul is steel: hard, slim, and bright;
Thrust it, o sister, through the night.

IV.

Signs? Signs? You ask for a sign?
These be the false signs that yet stir the mind
To spy for the true!

FRITZ LEIBER

The eye of the cat and the words of the madman,
Sudden, forsaken, meaningless words;
The cries of the screech owl, of shells, and far
  lightning,
Only seeming to come from the haunts of far souls;
The symbols bizarre of the mathematician,
Clear thought to him, a mad whisper to most;
The stones and the streets of dead, desert-hid cities,
Walked once by men commercial and civil,
Men up to the minute, by such and no others;
The brooding of mountains, the anger of oceans,
The lean wind, the cold spaces, the black suns
  beyond suns,
The howl of the wolf and the wing of the raven—
Those be the false signs,
Those be type of the thousand hints,
Which, sought for themselves, yield less than
  they seemed.
These be the true signs, if true signs there be:
The far darting of vision that comes with creation,
The quip of the great man sharp-tweaked by fate's
  fingers,
The last, doubtful hints on the great heap of
  knowledge,
Perched like strange birds that plot a strange flight;
The certainty born of practice and labour
But by what father none may know;
The slipping of meditant souls from earth bodies,
The pantherlike leap of imagination,
Second sight, far sight, beyond all suns seeing—
Those be the true signs, the signs of dark power,
The signs of the far way, if such signs there be.

The Demons of the Upper Air

$\mathcal{V}$.

Since light first fought with darkness
And the first created cat wailed down
The cry of chaos, now coherent,
From the new-risen, inky walls of Niffleheim,
We have been.
Old are we as the elder gods,
Yet not as they.
We strive not, boisterous,
To raise firmaments
But fly, black-winged, above;
They make the hearty music of the spheres—
We, the shrill, soaring overtones.
The windswept, icy mountaintops of mind
Show tracks of our sharp claws.
Both over raging war and striving peace
Our wing beat sounds;
Ultima Thule is our perching place,
For to the uttermost black bound of things
Our squadrons strive.
Ghosts are we but with skeletons of steel.
As mists are we, yet in our loins a seed
That laughs at barrenness.
The present grips the future with our claws,
Forgotten facts ride forward on our wings,
And inspiration's first faint harmonies
Sound in our songs, while eerie, far-off things
Call out to beg us bring them down to earth.
No one so deaf to miss our whispering,
No realm so lightless but our shadows fall;

Ho, wild, unrul'd allies upon the earth,
We are your friends who ride the icy nights,
We are the demons of the upper air.

VI.

Ho, tramper on the road below,
I spy the end toward which you go;
A little inn's across the hill,
Girls to sport with, wine to swill;
Chill is the way here in the air
And chill the part of you I bear.
Beyond the inn's a mountain tall,
Guarded by bastion and by wall,
Towers lift there from the snow,
Grimly gaze on those below;
Though manned by things with axe and mace,
Those towers are my perching place.
Beyond, a factory city's found
With costly suburbs snuggled round
And rich, sweet stench of luxury;
A mighty marching there I see,
Tuned to strong metal's martial din—
When I grin down on those rich things
I must beat swift my black bat wings—
For o'er that town the air is thin.
And still beyond's a dimmer way,
A castle dubious and dark,
A pit too deep for any day
To penetrate, and yet some spark
Lets me glimpse through the looming veil

The Demons of the Upper Air

An eyrie set above a dale.
Ho, tramper on the road below,
The way's not bad that you must go
And there is always enough air
To bear that part of you I bear;
But do not linger by the way,
Remember, I'm not in your pay.

VII.

Be these my words
To that which is higher,
To that which is darker,
To that which is swifter.
Be token, not worship,
Be spying, not trusting
The spirits of night
And the upper air riders.
Prayer-saken, ghost-ridden,
By earth-gods fear-shaken,
By elder things bidden,
I may not house with you
And yet I must seek you,
I may not school with you
And yet I must cry you.
Black loving and longing
To you be my token;
My soul has rid with you,
Its charger mistrusting;
My spirit has cried out
Your thin cries, dark lusting;

With you I have charged
In terror and pride
To riddle all riddles
In Asgardsride.
My words be a token
To lean souls swift riding;
My cry be a challenge
To evils time-biding.

VIII.

Out the frost-rimmed windows peer,
You who have arisen early,
Mind not cold for you may hear
A fanfare from the stratosphere.
"Ho, Brother! Is the way past Neptune clear?
And those strange beasts on the galactic rim—
Do they claw still the elder gods' last gate?
News of the airless monster whom kind fate
Drove once across the river none may swim?
What of the other creatures that we fear?
What stars tow now the planets they ruled late?
And he who went beyond—say, what of him?"
Eldritch words like these are flying,
Voices through the high air crying,
You whose sleep was too uneasy,
You may hear them, rising, dying.

GHOSTS

New built am I, yet haunted—
A prey for things from the elder years,
A penthouse smelling of plaster and paint,
Yet let only to ghosts,
By them sublet to ghost of ghosts.
Where are the new tenants?

THE RECOGNITION
of DEATH

I

It is a wonderful train ride
With the farms sliding by in the cold dusk
And animals grazing in the yellow sun
And little wooden—floored stations,
The boards brushed with frost or ordorous with
    rain,
And strange turbulent cities by night
With steel bridges over rivers reflecting lights
And vast mysterious depots.

But the conductor is always coming up behind me.
I can hear the click of his punch.
And I wonder if he will pass me by,
Or if he will take up my ticket
And I will have to get off and enter the landscape,
Become stationary forever.

FRITZ LEIBER

So I gaze more greedily
And talk to the person opposite
And rummage in my baggage,
And insincerely yawn,
And furiously think.

II

Death is my real friend,
Always doing things for my own good
Whether I like them or not.
He prods me toward the future,
He goads me to accomplishment,
He keeps reminding me of my unfulfilled
    potentialities,
Promises, hopes, intentions, and resloves.
He makes no promises.
He never threatens.
Yet he is eloquent.
If I lived ten thousand years
His voice would only be more urgent.

III

Death, a stern counsellor, is always at my elbow
    listening,
"The time is, was, and shall be," in his clipped accent
"You died ten years ago, tomorrow, now."
Often I have refused to see him, calling others to
    mask him from me.

THE RECOGNITION OF DEATH

Sloth and placidity are fat council men.
Their gross bodies easily cover his lean one.
But were I to put granite walls between us,
His words would be as true.
Forget mortal counsellors.
Death is the only true ally
He deals in verities.
He recognizes accomplishment.
He knows there are things he cannot kill,
Or, killing, must remember and so, make immortal.

IV

The killers creep towards me through the dark,
    red-smeared, with hate in their hearts.
But death is dignified and does not hate me,
The killers are ignorant and cruel.
But death knows all and regards me fairly.
The killers are not his agents—
It may happen that they will die at the hand of
    their intended victim.
Death will not kill me, but something that has
    life or movement—
A stone, a force, a micro-organism, the macro-
    organism.
Life will mangle me, and then death will
    befriend me.

CHALLENGE

To split a skull and laugh in furied glee at the red
    soul revealed,
To strike and fend where death doth sing in every
    tongue of steel,
Might make my life a precious article,
That now I barter as of little worth,
Trading rich days for doubtful coins
Which may or may not buy me one tomorrow
In the exchequer of the careless fates.
Fool's gold, farewell!

Satan, on guard!
No more you'll hoodwink me with dreams of
    future bliss.
Find other men to sell tomorrows to.
Those coins I sweat for—yours—I throw away!
You planned no payment, and I ask no pay.

NIGHT OF DEATH
An Introduction

Twilight advances, camouflaged by smoke;
The sooty walls grow sootier with gloom;
Without a sunset and without a breeze
Evening comes in on the metropolis.

Just so your ideas died; the great ideas
That are the blood of life, the rock on which
The house of life is built; just so they died,
A little at a time, monotonously.

The night springs up, the garish city night
Of neon, white hot tungsten, sodium,
Bright flowers of thin gases, shimmering glass,
Words burned alive and screaming in the sky.

Just so, inside your liquored, frightened mind,
The ideas no one dies for come to bloom,
The fake ideas, the robot, ghost ideas,
Sentimentalities of a machine.

THE GRAY MOUSER

I

Soft sandaled feet press lightly on the stones
That cobble Lankhmar' s mazy alleyways;
A grayish cloak melts in the river mist
That, like the ether of the alchemist,
Fumes round the corner from the nighted bays
To chill with sorcery men's blood and bones.
Only a bat whose sharp ears caught one sound
Knows that the Mouser is on business bound.

A jewel from Quarmall or a girl from Kled;
A caravel said to be docking soon;
A rune that Sheelba magicked from the dead;
Or a dread whisper from beyond the moon—
What man can name the thing the Mouser seeks
Or read the smile that links his swarthy cheeks?

THE GRAY MOUSER

II

The City thrusts black towers at the stars
And bars the forest back with morticed stones
And seals the scent of flowers in stone jars
And locks earth's secrets up in brass-clasped tomes.
No satyr may live there, no faun survive
The stench and clangor of each crowded street;
The white-fanged beasts of night cannot contrive
To gnaw an entrance through its black concrete.

Yet, 'mongst the gargoyles on its slated roofs,
One gray masked face leers down with living grin
That mocks the scurry of the city's floor;
Two gray gloved hands pry ope' the library's door,
And break the ponderous tomes and scribble in
Footnotes that give the lie to all proud proofs.

THE MIDNIGHT WALL

Poor five-foot girl, she's six feet underground.
At any rate, she'll never hear the sound
Of traffic and rude voices she'd despised,
Or shrill male English ego she realized
Was such a bitching blight on women there—
I always loved her gray, dry, silken hair.
She was a beaut, and tough, and ever living,
But not to any foe a bit forgiving.

Yet what is hate but love flipped on her face?
A posture for compassion, not disgrace.
And, incidentally, she was four-foot-ten—
A height appeals to most girl-centered men,
Black-haired Lolita, standing five feet tall,
Why do you glare out of the midnight wall?

5447 RIDGEWOOD COURT

Well, well, it's over—five-four-four-seven and the
   clover.
Oh, how we loved those days on Ridgewood Court—
The parties and the music and the art.
The young men shouting and the girls a-fever
And me a naïve sexual image-rover
And Jonquil never quite a sex believer.
And all such fucking fun, though seldom fucking—
White horses caprioling, nightmares bucking.

Upright piano crashing out folksong.
Mad, swashing saber-fights—once, not for long,
Our taped blades hit the kitchen light and arced it:
The white glare struck the face and forehead quaff
Of sisters named Naom and Nancy Smith;
And someone rushed to change his car where he'd
cross-parked it.

THE OTHER SIDE

And so it's over: Johnny and her tricks
Vanished the other side the River Styx
Her karma served and all her sins forgiven
Against herself, or 'gainst our Christian heaven.
But yet her pride remains—I think of that—
Her ebon stretch-pants and white leather hat,
Her gothic dreamings and her love so warm,
Her hate for every pig in uniform,

Her sturdy pelvis and her stubborn pride,
Her racialism, not to be denied,
Her love, her love, her love: that above all—
So vast within a girl not very tall;
Her love which over three and thirty years
Sustained me in this vale of acid tears.

PAST DRUID GUARDS

Past slender Druid guards we inward move,
Past woodly lives that sway above the ground.
Soft the leaves' kisses, softer the caress
Of grasses from the tender earth new-slipped.
Cool is the diamond dew on carmine-lipped,
Green-sepaled and green-hooded blooms that bless
Our haven, dear of sighs and murmurous sound,
By one more prayer its sanctity to prove.

And yet this grove that wraps our dreaming heart
Is but a bower in a terrible wild
Where shadowy, brooding figures stalk apart
Along a panorama storm cloud piled.
Now past our bower's quivering scrim we see
The galloping mirthless hordes of destiny.

THE VOICE OF MAN

When man first strode out of his ochered cave
A host of gods came with him from the dark:
Puissant guards with powers beyond the grave.
But light is cruel to gods; the awful spark
Of knowledge grew, and man must watch each die,
Until but one was left upon his throne,
And that one shrunken to a puerile lie,
And man must face the aching void alone.

In nature are strange, haunting cries that seem
To voice the very heart of solitude:
The mourning of the dove, the seahawk's scream,
Hoot of the owl through woods that drearly brood
Howl of the wolf under the sky's gray span;
Last of these lonely cries: the voice of man.

POOR LITTLE APE

Poor little ape, you're sick again tonight.
Has the shrill, fretful chatter fevered you?
Was it a dream lion gave you such a fright?
And did the serpent Fear glide from the slough?
You cough, you moan, I hear your small teeth grate.
What are those words you mutter as you toss?
War, torture, guilt, revenge, crime, murder, hate?
I'll stroke your brow, poor little ape—you're cross.

Far wiser beasts under far older stars
Have had your sickness, seen their hopes denied,
Sought God, fought Fate, pounded against the bars,
And like you, little ape, they some day died.
The bough swings in the wind, the night is deep.
Look at the stars, poor little ape, and sleep.

SANTA MONICA BEACH
AT SUNSET

White gulls show black 'gainst sunset sky,
So distant that I hear no cry—
A quivering troop in silhouette,
Black flakes from smouldering cigarette
Driven by fitful indoor wind,
Their spots are brownianly assigned;
Phone wires are bars—the birds are notes
In symphony of scattering motes.

How spectral silent the wide beach!
Waves' roar, gulls' screams can no more reach
Than blast of bombs across the sea
Can come eight thousand miles to me,
Or screams of charring humans reach—
Yet why so spectral in the beach?

1959:
the Beach at Santa Monica

At any one time
A man may see too much,
Feel too much,
Know too much.
Too much knowledge swirls the mind,
Too much feeling twists,
Too much striving paralyzes
Listen to the birds,
Listen to the wind,
Listen to the sea.
See the ocean's white spiders
Die in the spumy fringe.
Observe the heeling gulls,
Black flakes of coming night.
Watch for the green flash
Of the vanishing sun.
See the golden stalks of the jets
Grow in the afterglow.
Walk in the sound of the surf.
Study the constant moon

FRITZ LEIBER

As she walks west and east
And south and north,
Marking her bounds.
Strengthen yourself in sensation,
Brace yourself against your atoms.
The world is firm.
The universe is sure.
Return again to this knowledge.

OTHER
WORKS

THE MYSTERY OF THE JAPANESE CLOCK

ON THE TABLE that is at the head of my couch and stands against the wall I have a digital electric clock from Japan made of an orange plastic that verges on vermilion. Its entire front is transparent, revealing a dull black surface in which there are two windows. Through the tiny one to the left I see a rapid whirl of red and white, indicating that the central horizontal shaft of the clock is rotating obediently to the current. The window on the right, much larger and very wide, shows the big, white-on-black digits that tell the time. The numbers ride on two sets of panels, one for the hours, the other for the minutes, which are evenly nested (circularly stacked) around two wheels, which in turn are geared to the central shaft. It takes the minute wheel, of course, one hour to make a single rotation, during which all the sixty numerals from 00 to 59 are in turn displayed. Each panel is divided into an upper and a lower half, horizontally hinged at the middle. As the minute wheel slowly turns, the upper half of the panel in view (which shows the upper half of the number being displayed) creeps slowly forward and down until it escapes from an inconspicuous restraining tab at the top and falls over very quickly, with a barely audible dull click, revealing on its reverse face the lower half of the next number to be displayed and bringing into view the upper half of that same next number. A minute later the process is repeated, and so on until the minute wheel has made one complete turn. At this point the upper panel half on the hour wheel, which has been creeping forward sixty times as slowly, escapes from its restraining tab and falls over, revealing the numeral of the next hour, exactly at the same time as the upper panel half of the 59 falls over, revealing the 00. The two dull clicks coming together make a noticeably louder and easily audible one.

Actually the hinged hour and minute panels are arranged around their wheels very much like the hinged and weighted levers in the most popular form of perpetual motion machine, reinvented again and again over the centuries. As their wheel revolves, the hinged levers fall over and stop with their weights extended farther from the wheel's center, which is supposed to keep it going forever. But there are always more weights on the opposite side, waiting to fall over, unfortunately.

My Japanese clock could readily be a twenty-four hour one, having a 13 instead of 1 PM with 24 its midnight, but it is old fashioned in this respect. Twelve hour panels with a small AM superscription in their upper left-hand corners are followed by twelve with a PM subscript, lower left-hand corner. During the beginning of each hour, each minute numeral slowly creeps down below the hour numeral and then seems to jump up level again with the hour numeral and change into the next minute numeral. Of course this *is* an illusion: The dropping panel has vanished one number and revealed another beginning its downward creep. While toward the end of each hour, when the hour panel has crept almost all the way down itself, the minute panels start above, and their downward creep looks like an effort to catch up. At the moment when the hour changes, both numerals seem to jump up together. All of these small changes of level are readily observed, though not at all obtrusive.

At the right end of the clock is a large knob shaped like a thick poker chip flat against the end. By turning it you can turn the minute and hour wheels to set the clock. Of course it must only be turned one way, ahead; there's no way to make the panels reverse themselves and fall upward except to turn the clock upside down—and even this wouldn't get the panels behind their restraining tab again. So if the clock is a few minutes fast you must turn it through a full twenty-four hours, AM and PM both, to set it right. Or you can turn off its current (unplug it) long enough for time to catch up with it.

That one big knob is the only outside control on the clock at all—a nice simple setup, pleasantly neat. On the back are some small slits, presumably to ventilate the small electric motor. Underneath is a nameplate with the model number and so forth. While underneath the small whirly window is COPAL, the name of the company that sells the clock.

FOR A LONG while that was all I understood about the clock—and that it kept excellent time, of course. But then I began to wonder vaguely about the hour and the minute panels falling so precisely together at the end of each hour—the panel for the preceding hour and the 59 panel dropping simultaneously every hour. At first my wondering was just a fleeting thought, gone almost as soon as it arrived—a quick smile and headshake whenever I chanced to see the panels fall together, in recognition of such phenomenal accuracy. But then I began to think about it a little at odd moments, and I slowly became convinced that such accuracy wasn't just phenomenal; it was downright impossible. That the minute and the hour wheels geared to the central shaft should revolve with great precision, a precision as great as the whirling shaft got from the precise alternations of the current—that I could understand. It was a good clock, yes. But that the panels should continue to fall exactly together day after day, month after month (and I suppose year after year—I'd had the clock two years), especially when you considered that just a little uneven wear on the restraining tabs, or on the panels themselves, would throw them out of synchronicity—no, that was too good to be true. Granted, the Japanese and the plastics were good, but not that good. There had to be some trick to it. There had to be something more than electricity and gears connecting the falls of the two panels.

At that moment I was at last driven to take up the clock carefully, holding it level, and look again closely at the dull black, white-numbered face of which I'd once thought I'd seen and understood everything. The clock happened to be nearing the end of an hour. Almost at once I made a new discovery: The hour panel had *two* restraining tabs—one at the top and in the middle, like the minute panels, the other toward the top but coming in from the side, from the inside where the minute panels were. And it was this tab that was now (nearing the hour change) keeping the hour panel from falling—the top wasn't helping at all; the hour panel had already escaped from that.

Hard on the heels of the first, I made a second discovery: The dull black hour and minute panels were not alike; the latter had a black ear at the top that went out on the inside, the hour panel side—nothing at all conspicuous truly, just a short extension of its dull uniform black surfaces.

And then I made the third discovery, the discovery which gave me the connection I'd been hunting for between minute and the hour panels, the something more than gears and electricity linking them together so that the one could have an effect on the other: The ears on the minute panels were pushing out the second tab so that it covered the edge of the hour panel, restraining it from falling.

The 59 panel came up and finally fell. The 00 panel had no ear on it! There was nothing pushing out the second restraining tab. So it sprang back and the old hour panel fell and fell so almost simultaneously with the 59 panel as to fool the eye—for the events of this short paragraph took place far, far more swiftly than it takes to tell them, or even speed-read them. The louder click here merged three swiftly successive sounds—the minute panel falling, the side tab springing back, and the hour panel falling.

Now since the 59 and the other minute panels coming just before it had ears, while the 00 panel didn't, there had to be a point at which the earless minute panel gave way to the eared ones. It turned out to be the 35 panel. From 00 through 33, the hour panel was restrained only by its top tab. From 35 on, it was also restrained by the side tab, and could creep out from under the top tab at any time without falling. (Actually the eared 35 panel pushed over the tab while the earless 34 panel was still showing—about when the 34 panel dropped, in fact. During the last fifteen minutes or so of each hour, only the side tab restrained it. Actually it had fallen forward a very short distance to lie against the side tab only.)

I'd like to say, incidentally, that during all this process of careful handling and intent inspection of (and step-by-step thinking about) my Japanese clock, I was conscious of a mounting tension and dry-throated excitement that must be, I thought, except for the absence of fear, very like that experienced by a person trying to defuse a live time-bomb or figure out the mechanism of a booby trap. I was reminded of Nigel Balchin's excellent World War II novel, *The Small Back Room*, and Masterpiece Theater's TV series *UXB*. In Balchin's novel the climactic problem was defusing a booby-trap bomb disguised as a large red flashlight. The discovery there that this bomb had two fuses that had to be neutralized before it could be moved or even joggled struck me as analogous to my own discovery of the two tabs restraining the fall of the hour panels.

In any case, my heightened awareness, whatever its explanation, led me to new discoveries about my clock and further problems.

Looking through the bottom of the big window, you could see the short equal space between the last four or five panels which had just fallen—the distances by which they failed to overlap each other completely—and get an idea of how they were evenly nested all the way around the wheels. Like a deck of cards fanned out around a cylinder—actually, the analogy is fairly close numerically for the minute wheel, since there are fifty-two cards to a deck and sixty minutes to an hour. The hour panels were definitely a little farther apart from each other than were the minute panels, as though there were actually only fifty-two of them (or maybe forty-eight—a pinochle deck!) instead of sixty.

That frivolous thought brought me squarely up against the new problem—hit me between the eyes with it, you might say (I really was doing a lot of squinting at the clock): There should be only twenty-four hour panels, twelve AMs and twelve PMs, nested around the hour wheel. But if that were really the case, then the hour panels would be much farther from each other than the minute panels were from each other—two and a half times as far, to be exact—and that much difference in spacing would be very, rather than barely, noticeable. Also the white hour numerals would crawl down the face of the clock two and a half times as far before they fell, and seem to jump up the same greater distance when they finally did, and that much unevenness would again be very noticeable—the face of the clock would look cockeyed at times. But it didn't. What was the explanation?

My first guess was that the hour wheel was geared to make only one rotation in two days and that there were two sets of twenty-four hour panels and numerals. That way they'd come spaced as I'd observed them, forty-eight hour panels—the pinochle theory, I named it. Too bad, I thought, they couldn't use five sets of twelve panels, then they'd come out spaced exactly like the minute since five times twelve is sixty—but then the AM and PM sets couldn't be made to come in the proper alternating sequence.

Actually it turned out that my guess was both right and wrong. There were indeed forty-eight hour panels and numerals, but the hour wheel took only a day to rotate. Put that way it sounds impossible, doesn't it? I still had a lot to learn about the clock.

At this point I did something I'd been rather reluctant to do: I took up the clock and rotating the knob at its end, ran it ahead through a full twenty-four-hour cycle. I was reluctant because it was always a bit of a bother resetting the clock and because it didn't seem to be quite playing the game—the game being (as I realized now) to find out as much as possible about the natural operation of the clock simply by observing it without tampering with it in any way or, of course, going inside it. Well, resetting the clock was part of its natural operations; it certainly wasn't tampering with it, I told myself.

Watching the two sets of panels fall as the clock went through a speeded-up twenty-four-hour cycle, I soon made a discovery I hadn't at all anticipated. I'd been hoping to notice some little difference between the individual panels of the first twenty-four hour set and those of the second. What I discovered was that at about twenty minutes after each hour, an hour panel fell, revealing an identical hour panel beneath it— behind the 1 AM there was another 1 AM, then cane the 2 AM, another 2 AM, the 3 AM, and so on. Very tricky!— for you'd never see the fall of the first hour panel at twenty-after unless you were watching the hour panel closely at that moment and even if you did, you'd be inclined to doubt your eyes, for the effect of the twenty-after change was that nothing had happened—an hour panel had been replaced by an identical one. Yes, very tricky—stealthy, in fact. The things clocks did when you weren't watching them—and even when you were. Like card tricks in a way.

It also fitted with what I knew about the top restraining tab of the hour panels. The second hour panel would have crept out from under it and fallen in turn at forty after or so, but by then the side tab which had come in at 34 was restraining it.

And, of course, the whole reason for these extra panels was to space the hour panels more closely and so make them more conformable to the minute panels, so that they wouldn't crawl down and jump tip the face of the clock to an irritatingly greater degree. Well, at any rate, the pinochle theory was proved, though in an unexpected fashion.

I've mentioned that my Japanese clock keeps very good time over the weeks and months—so very good that early on it became a fad of mine to get it set as precisely as I could in correspondence with the time as given over the telephone by the Time of Day service. It was a real thrill to hear the recorded female voice say, for example, "The time is five o'clock exactly," and then hear the recorded *beep* and (almost at the same time) see the two panels fall together, revealing five and zero-zero, while hearing the accompanying rather loud dull click. I'll spare you, at least for now, all the details of the fussy manipulations involved in getting the clock set as closely as possible to telephone time, my supreme authority. It involved putting the clock a few minutes ahead, stopping it by unplugging it as soon as a minute panel fell revealing a new minute, waiting for telephone time to catch up with the stalled clock, and plugging it in the moment the *beep* sounded for the arrival of the temporarily frozen minute.

Once my Japanese clock was accurately set by phone time, I became interested in how well it held to that time. Did it gain or lose a trifle each day?—one or the other seemed likely to me—with these tiny errors adding up over the weeks and months into larger and more obvious ones. I had the general impression that my Japanese clock kept pretty close to phone time in the long run, but just how close, I wanted to know. A passion for measuring things to the second seized me—telephone time wasn't altogether satisfactory here, since it only *beeped* every ten seconds; it measured time in ten-second chunks only, you might say, just as my Japanese clock measured it only in minute chunks. So I had to make use of my Caravelle wristwatch because it has a sweep second hand.

Now the Caravelle wristwatch is the economy workhorse of Bulova, with durability and high resistance to water and shocks its other chief selling points. It corresponds to Timex. There was a time when I didn't realize that. You see, about fifteen years earlier, rather late in both our lives, my mother gave me a Caravelle as a birthday present. Up to that point

I'd had no faith in wristwatches. After a few days or months you dropped them on a cement floor or plunged them into hot dish water, or banged them, together with your wrist, against a door jamb, and thereafter they weren't any good. But in spite of any number of incidents of that sort, this Caravelle kept on going month after month, year after year, gaining a constant ten seconds a day with a sort of unquenchable enthusiasm, forever hurrying and keeping a little ahead of things, never falling behind and never failing, a regular Horatio Alger, Jr., of a watch, thoroughly reliable if you reset it once or twice a week, so that when the mainspring finally went, I hunted around the jewelry counters for a long while to find out where I could get it repaired before discovering that I ought to have inquired at household goods or notions or my local drugstore. Well, it's probably a healthy thing for a son somewhat to overvalue gifts from his mother.

The Caravelle which I loyally bought to replace it wasn't quite as good. It lost about twenty-five seconds a day, but it did so with great regularity, so if you reset it every day it was as good as the other for all practical purposes. I could certainly trust its second hand for what I intended to do with it—twenty-five seconds lost a day works out to one an hour, nothing to worry about.

What I did with the second hand was this: I'd wait for the fall of a minute panel and dial Time of Day. Then while listening to its spoken and beeped messages, I'd closely watch the sweep second hand of my Caravelle travel around the dial, keeping my wrist close to the face of my Japanese clock so that out of the corner of my eye I could watch the fall of the next panel. (Of course I also listened for the dull click that made, but it was pretty faint and easily lost in the background noise, such as a fire or ambulance siren, a passing airplane,

or voices in the hall.) While this was going on, I'd mentally
locate or "place" the phone beeps on my wristwatch dial. I'd
say to myself, "They're coming three seconds after the tens,"
(meaning by the 10s the 10, 20, 30, 40, 50, and "minute
exactly" markings on the wristwatch dial) or "They're coming
one second after the fives," (the 5, 15, 25, 35, 45, and 55 markings) and I'd also keep in mind which beep was coming next,
the "and thirty seconds" or whatever, so that if she hung up
before the next panel fell (as sometimes happened, I suppose
when she was getting too many calls at once, poor overworked
machine), I could keep on echoing her beeps in my mind and
saying to myself which each beep was, so that I'd be able to
time the next panel's fall as accurately as if she were still on
the line and doing her stuff.

In other words, I was temporarily transferring phone time
to my wristwatch dial, so that I'd be able to break up its ten-
second hunks into seconds and measure a panel's fall with that
much greater accuracy. Of course, once I'd done that transfer, I
didn't really need to keep on listening to phone time until it cut
off, but I got a kick out of being able to attend to three things
at once: Japanese clock, Caravelle wristwatch, and phone
time—the old urge to emulate Napoleon dictating three dis-
patches at once, or Reti playing forty blindfold games simultaneously. Moreover, it felt good—a sort of quickening and quivering excitement—to stretch my awareness that way, to keep it
hovering effectively over as wide and diverse a field as possible.

In any case, I had done what I'd set out to do. I now had
the pleasure of seeing directly with my own eyes exactly how
many seconds my Japanese clock was running fast or slow by
telephone time, and perhaps an even greater pleasure to look
forward to: that of knowing how little my clock's own time
varied over the weeks and months.

But right at this point a really very strange problem slowly arose. After hardly varying a second a day by phone time for three or four days, or even a week, my clock would suddenly lose or gain ten or fifteen seconds overnight. The next day's observation might confirm this loss or gain, or even show a greater one, but more likely it would indicate a return to the earlier figure—a wiping out of yesterday's sudden loss or gain. This happened several times. It bothered me that it wasn't any sort of *steady* loss or gain, but rather small yet sizable variations which tended to correct themselves, given time—over long periods it *did* seem to keep very good time. I had all sorts of ideas about what might be causing it. Perhaps I was observing some flaw in telephone time, some mis-setting of the tapes that gave the Time of Day messages. Perhaps there were sudden small interruptions or variations in the alternating current coming through the wires to govern my clock, variations which did not also affect the Time of Day messages. Perhaps...it was, as I said before, really very strange.

Incidentally, I use the word "strange" here partly in the sense that Hamlet did when Horatio said the ghost was strange and the melancholy prince responded, "And therefore as a stranger give it welcome"—that is, strange as referring to some thing or person coming from outside, from another realm, a far-off unfamiliar country. As a writer of horror stories, I've had to bear the criticism that we over-use words such as "strange," "weird," "eerie," "uncanny" and of course the current *bete noir*, "eldritch," so it's rather fun to watch Shakespeare doing the same thing in *Hamlet*: HORATIO: "'Tis strange." HAMLET, topping him, "'Tis very strange." HORATIO, topping him in turn: "Oh day and night, but this is wondrous strange." HAMLET (now that Shakespeare by repetition has got us thinking about that sometimes trite word): "And therefore as a stranger," etc. By the by, that "wondrous strange" of Horatio's picks up on his earlier reaction to the ghost ("It harrows me with fear and wonder") and in so doing provides us with an explanation of the power of the supernatural horror story (SEE my essay, "Terror, Mystery, Wonder," *World Fantasy Awards, Volume Two*).

But I was talking about the possibility of my Japanese clock and the time it kept being affected by influences from outside it and beyond, and how I was reaching far out for explanations. At this point it occurred to me that although my clock kept very good time by the hour, it provided no check on how long its minutes were—the times between the droppings of the right hand panels; it had no equivalent of a sweep second hand. So I decided to measure its minutes by my wristwatch. Checking out a whole hour seemed a formidable task, so I'd start with those times when something more than a single panel falling was happening to the clock, such as when the minute and hour panels fell at once, or when that tricky identical-twin hour-panel fell around twenty after, or the eared 35 panel pushed in the second tab restraining the hour panels—those mechanical happenings night affect minute length.

It was a lucky guess. Very soon I'd discovered that the thirty-fourth minute on the clock, the time between the falls of the 33 and 34 panels, was 77 seconds long. This happened anytime I checked that particular minute. It happened every hour, AM or PM, ack emma or pip emma, no difference. While the first minute (between 00 and 01) was generally 53 seconds long. There even seemed to be a rogue minute near twenty after: the twenty second, some sixty-nine seconds long. This came as a great surprise to me, almost as if it were a transgression of natural law, though it shouldn't have. Those minute panels weren't so all-fired accurate after all; I'd just assumed they were. And an over-long or over-short minute isn't the sort of thing you'd really notice. Any minute seems terribly long as soon as you concentrate on watching it out, waiting for it to end—a watched pot never boils, etc. So long as the minute panels kept dropping fairly regularly, you'd never think to question their accuracy.

At least I could see how this could explain the sudden gains and losses of time that had been bothering me. If I called Time of Day, say, just after the thirty-fourth minute, my Japanese clock would check out slow; just after the change-of-hour, fast.

A noteworthy point here. I usually call Time of Day just after five in the morning, because I called Weather at five, since that was when they put the first new weather forecast for the day on the phone. As long as I kept doing that, my Japanese clock would keep in step with phone time. But then, suppose—as did happen now and then—I called Time of Day just before the hour or especially just after the long thirty-fourth or twenty-second minutes? My clock would have lost ten seconds or so overnight! And then suppose that next day I returned—naturally enough—to my practice of calling Time of Day just after the hour. My clock would have gained back the ten seconds or so it had lost, and again overnight! Incidents like this would explain my clock's self-correcting tendency which puzzled me so strangely.

What had kept all of this hidden from me so long, of course, I realized next, was that all the sixty mismatched giant and dwarf minutes must add up very closely indeed to a normal hour of thirty-six hundred seconds, the shorts balancing out the longs, or else my inscrutable Japanese clock couldn't possibly have pretended to be keeping such very good time.

I decided then and there I just had to gird my loins, check this out once and for all by measuring the length of each of the sixty minutes, although what I proposed to do was beginning to seem suspiciously like work, even scientific research of a trivial sort.

So I laid my wristwatch beside my Japanese clock, both in a good light, so I could concentrate on the dial of the former while seeing the fall of the latter's panels from the corner of my eye, whether I heard them or not. No time wasted, of course, shifting my gaze between digits and dial. For the last few seconds before each fall I was watching the dial directly and the digits peripherally. I'd know for sure which second I was in when the panel fell; a second's a long time tackled that way. Then I'd have forty seconds or so to record my reading and get ready for the next observation. (But thank goodness I didn't have to manage the phone too!) I set my pencil and pad (with the numbers one to sixty penciled in columns, with a dash and blank space following each), my coffee mug, cigarettes, matches, and ashtray easy to hand, waited for the hour's start, took a deep breath or two, and began.

My apprehensions of having to work were justified. By the hour's end I was breathing a bit hard and even sweating a little. My sympathies to all people who have to watch dials or gauges and to all musicians and dancers who have to count measures before coming in exactly on the beat!—those are no easy tasks, believe me, I now know from experience. I also know how long it takes me to light a match—about seven seconds—or a cigarette—about the same—or dial the shortest seven-digit telephone number—about six—or the longest—about sixteen (pushbutton "dialing" is so much faster); I had to do *something* to fill up the interminable middles of all those sixty minutes.

I even missed one minute completely, the thirty-first, because I got caught short and answering this minor call of nature took a bit longer than I'd anticipated. Later I faked it in my records by making it sixty seconds long—a reasonable enough assumption but still an assumption in the game I was playing. Oh well, I told myself with outrageous hopefulness, no piece of scientific research is truly real unless one figure is faked, just as it's not a real party until someone spills a drink. (But only *one* figure, mind you! "I give a dog *one* bite," etc. Ah, but it's simple and neat and nice to live—and think—by platitudes and aphorisms rather than exact observations and measurements! Budding scientists, be warned!—or have your worst suspicions about non-scientists confirmed!)

Also, beginning with the twenty-third second, I sharpened my measurements by recording several minutes of "so many and a half" seconds, ten in all (again I was looking for something extra to do to fill in time); in my records I later made half of these the longer figure and half the shorter—that way they'd add up to the same total for the hour and keep the figure of one-half out of my tables.

What I was recording, of course, was the number of seconds between the end of a minute by phone time, transferred to and being viewed on my wristwatch dial, and the fall of the corresponding clock panel; later on I translated these figures to minute lengths.

Here's the record I finally got: the table for the length of each minute on my Japanese clock (00 could also be called 60, of course, but it columns out neater the first way):

00-6010-6020-6230-5540-5950-59
01-5511-6021-6031-6041-5951-61

The Mystery of the Japanese Clock

02-6012-6122-6932-5942-5952-59
03-5913-6023-5633-6143-5853-59
04-6014-5924-6134-7644-6154-59
05-5815-5825-6435-5845-6255-59
06-5816-6026-5836-6046-6156-61
07-6017-5827-5837-6347-5757-62
08-5918-5928-6138-5948-6158-61
09-6019-5929-5939-5949-6159-56

Well, right at the start you'll notice a discrepancy: Earlier the 00-01 minute turned out to be always 53 seconds long, while here it's 55. All I can say is: That's how it was this run. While the 33-34 minute turned out to be 76 instead of 77 seconds long. Same excuse.

Glancing at the figures, it's difficult to tell offhand how they'll add up. The giant minutes boast a monster 76-second one and a 69, while the best the dwarfs can muster is two 55s. On the other hand, there are sixteen minutes a second short and eight two minutes short, while only twelve and three minutes are one and two seconds longer respectively. (That's where the minus minutes forge ahead—in the number of them—and catch up on the pluses.)

The gratifying point to me to discover was that all the sixty minutes together add up to 3596 seconds—only four fewer than 3600, the true number of them in an hour. I'd told myself beforehand that, as far as I could figure it out, they must add up that way. And they did. The minus four reflect nothing more than a tendency on my part to call them short rather than long in doubtful cases—which might easily have put my count further out. The result was as good as could be expected, considering human reaction time and general fallibility.

FRITZ LEIBER

With a last intent look at her broad, white-figured, enigmatic black face framed in fiery orange, I began the long process of detaching my attention from my Japanese clock.

———

I WROTE MOST of the foregoing four years ago, in December of 1977, and then set it aside. I'd done it to test or demonstrate how clearly I—a writer of fiction, chiefly, fantasy fiction and science-fiction at that—could do a piece of purely descriptive and deductive writing, following a trail of logical reasoning, and incidentally celebrate a minor mystery in my life that I had been able to solve by my own efforts. I've enjoyed detective stories all my life, but never been able to write a book-length one satisfactorily although I've had at least one serious try—perhaps that had something to do with it.

A year later I showed it to my son, a professional philosopher, as a curiosity and for what light it threw upon my own mental processes—it seemed the closest things in my writing to the sort of rigorous thinking a scientist or philosopher does. I'd once wanted to be a philosopher myself and spent at it an abortive year of graduate work at the University of Chicago in 1933-34—later I'd been glad when my son tackled the same field successfully.

My son made use of the Japanese clock-piece in an article, "Fritz Leiber and Eyes" (*Starship*, Summer, 1979), he wrote about me and my works. And later still—in September of 1980, in fact, he published his first science-fiction novel, *Beyond Rejection*. Those happenings and other considerations decided me to finish my little essay and seek its publication.

I began by going back in my daybooks over the time immediately preceding my writing the Japanese-clock piece. I soon discovered that I had been puzzling sporadically and ineffectively about it and the sort of time it kept, especially as compared with phone time, gradually becoming a bit obsessed with the problems involved, for a period of at least six or eight months rather than the short time (and rather effortless, efficient reasoning!) my writing implied.

Already in May 1977 I am making frequent entries of how slow or fast the clock is by phone time. In July a week's daily entries consist of nothing but the date and that single item, which begins to sound like a symptom of some sort. Actually, these months were a most anxious and ineffectual period for me. I was trying unsuccessfully to write the full scenario of an impossibly super-super film about my characters Fafhrd and the Gray Mouser. At the same time I was hunting almost as ineffectively for a new apartment to replace one that was becoming much too uncomfortable and small and which I stood to lose soon in any case. I recall I became so jittery that I began my days by playing over old chess and even back-gammon games (both book games and my own) to steady my nerves before really starting the day, and to avoid attacks of the munchies, at least early in the morning.

Then in September I said a conclusive "*No!*" to the whole film project and at the same time unexpectedly discovered an apartment that was everything I'd wanted, and rented and moved into it. While early in the month there is the decisive entry: "There *must* be variations of as much as ten seconds in phone or electric-clock time. Clock or phone varies frequently by as much as ten seconds from *hour to hour*." (Sounds almost as if, under extreme tensions, I was beginning to think that Time itself was coming unraveled, the fabric of reality falling apart, and complete disorientation setting in!)

I should say at this point that *orientation* has always been one of the prime objects of my daybooks, which I began in

FRITZ LEIBER

December 1972 just after ending three years of heavy-drinking-for-tranquilization. A writer of fiction soon learns that it helps a story along if early on you tell the reader *who* and *what* it's about, and *where* and *when* it's happening, and *how*, and maybe, eventually, if you can, *why*. It's even more important that a person regularly answer those same questions about himself, reaffirming or bravely changing the answers when necessary—and there the clear mind of morning, stars, the sky and water, yes, even clocks, are helpful. Each daily day-book entry would almost always begin with the recounting of a visit to the roof before dawn to observe the stars, moon, and planets in their courses (or in absence of those the vagaries of San Francisco's fog and other weather), a getting-in-touch with the city and the cosmos and their rhythms and with the background or field of all rhythms—Time; it was an obvious and natural step to make daily calls to Weather and Time of Day an additional habit. Also, my recovery from alcoholism had been marked by a growing interest in and concern about small numbers—something to occupy my mind, perhaps, in the absence of the boozing glow. Early on I remember writing the prime numbers between one and one hundred (1, 2, 3, 5, 7, 11, etc., through 97) on a convenient blackboard at Garden-Sullivan Hospital very early in the morning to mystify or instruct the chance passer-by. I counted my small change over, segregating the different coins in different pockets—a habit I still have. The garden of that same hospital had a circular walk traversed by two crosswalks; I tried to walk it in all possible patterns of turns and returns. I tore paper matches from packets of twenty or thirty so as to create different symmetrical patterns in the course of a day's smoking. (Art found its way into *that* inanity; I pretended the matches were actors and tried always to keep the stage as they exited one by one, especially when there were as few as seven or eight left—who'd be the last left on and where?) A bit later on I even made a mobile of the five Platonic solids, inscribing the fifty faces with different astrological, alchemical, meteorological, and magic symbols. I played around in my mind with phone and license-plate numbers. It's a wonder I didn't become a convert to numerology somewhere along the line. Synchronicity, anyone?

All this concern with counting and exact placement in space and time likely gave an added and almost ritualistic importance for me to the Mystery of the Japanese Clock.

The 100 sheets of *Daybook 37* were sufficient for my entries and notes that nervous and abominable summer: May, June, July, August, and half of September all in one grubby wirebound notebook. While *Daybooks 38, 39, 40,* and *41* only take us into January of 1978, a month a book, recording my honeymoon with my new apartment (I got so sentimental that I personified the four-room thing and thought of myself as buying it presents), notes on the two novelettes I immediately wrote, ending a long dry spell ("Black Glass" and "The Mer She"), and several snippets of thought on the electric clock problem, such as (Oct. 8) "Really hold accurate when they do, don't they?—that Japanese clock and the phone tone. Wonder which varies when they do?," (Oct. 9) "My checking-electric-clock-by-phone behavior illustrates my reverence for— no, rather my commitment to—science," and finally on Nov. 5th, without fanfare, the actual word-for-word beginning of this article you have been reading, filling seven daybook-pages with careful final-draft writing.

I think it's significant that this article is just about the only piece of writing I ever began word by word in my daybook, trying to make the object I was writing about grow up real and clear in the mind's inner darkness with as few words as possible and just the right ones connecting them like atoms into molecules, taking advantage of the new-minted freshness of early morning visions and ideas, when the mind's been raked smooth by sleep and dreams, not scrawled over everywhere with the day's graffiti, as it is by evening, so there's hardly any clear space in which to operate creatively.

My usual daybook style leans toward ellipsis and epithets, Pepysian dodges and self-jokes, dates, names, and figures, double nouns and other hyphenations, nonsentences generally, and pet abbreviations of no value. (If yest is yesterday, you know who tod and tom are, while ton's tonight.) There are lots of symbols—I delight in their looks, they make me feel scholarly and mysterious; last year I learned the Greek, Arabic, and Hebrew alphabets in my daybooks, buying a stub pen for the last of these, though I doubt I could scribble off more than the Greek today—but illustrations tend to appear only when three topics come up: astronomy, sex, and high-rise San Francisco architecture; those last mostly tall, slender rectangles with notes on materials, storeys, number and style of windows per floor, and whether there's a flag on top, or other roof oddities; but those buildings are the Stonehenge of my rooftop astronomy, the supercilious and severe aristocrats of the roof-top world.

So you see why I think it's significant that I began my article there.

And now to bid a final farewell to—No! by Chronos, Saturn, and Urania! let's have another go at her! let's watch her through an hour just once more! Three years have passed since the last time, I'm in *Daybook 72* instead of *40*. I've the experience I gained from that first run and from writing this piece about the Japanese clock. And I've a new weapon to use on her this time, a sister digital timepiece to test her against, a Casio ML-71 Electronic Calculator & Watch that gains only a second a week on phone time (I've tested it over three months); it's much easier to watch seconds on than a wristwatch dial, perhaps this time we'll get deeper under her renowned black-visaged inscrutability! peel away another layer of her mystery. But be ready for anything.

So set the calculator just in front of the clock, both their display windows in a good light for easy viewing. Set out the pad with one to sixty on it, two sharpened pencils, cigarets, ashtray, and lighter (another new feature), and the steaming coffee. Hide that table with the results of the first run three years ago!—don't want to start checking them against each other until the second run's over. And this time set the phone off the hook—that's one interruption can be headed off—and remember to empty the bladder. Anything else? All right, let's go!

Well, it's good I told myself to be ready for anything, because almost from the start I got the feeling that the figures I was getting this time were very different from those I'd got three years ago—early on there was a short sequence of long minutes that I didn't remember at all from the first run. I told myself to ignore that and just concentrate on making each observation as it came along—God knows I had time and enough to get ready for each of them. But I couldn't help remembering the "giant" second at 22, and it never did turn up. I did note the fall of the extra hour panel and it flustered me; I'd forgotten to expect it. About the only reassurance I got was that 34 turned out again to be a very long minute.

I did keep my cool enough to make notes of the minute in which the extra hour panel fell—the twentieth—and the number of cigarettes I smoked during that run—only four, lighting the last in the fifty-eighth minute. I was neither breathing hard nor sweating. And I hadn't been caught short, though I was relieved to be able to make a little trip now.

I wasted no time transforming my figure to minute lengths so I'd be able to view the extent of the disaster, recalling how I'd been flown in a light plane around Mt. St. Helen's black crater and devastated surrounds a month earlier.

```
00-5710-5920-6130-6040-6150-61
01-5311-6021-5931-5541-6051-65
02-5612-5822-5932-6142-6252-60
03-6313-6023-6133-5843-5853-61
04-6314-6124-5934-7944-5754-55
05-6315-6125-6335-5745-5955-60
06-5616-6026-6036-5946-5756-64
07-5817-5927-5637-6147-5857-59
08-5918-6228-6738-6148-6058-53
09-5919-6129-6139-6249-5859-65
```

To summarize catastrophe: Only *five* minutes in the second run have the same length in seconds they did in the first. You'd think there'd have to be more, just by chance! All the others, fifty-five of 'em, differ by varying amounts up to ten seconds—the "giant" twenty-second minutes of sixty-nine seconds, which disappeared completely, becoming a fifty-niner with no biggies near her. None of the "runs" of like-valued minutes in either table—five and four fifty-nine second minutes in table one, an early three sixty-three second minutes in table two, which tipped me off something was going wrong—are repeated in the other; in fact, there appears to be a diabolic tendency to go off in the opposite direction in those cases.

This is supposed to be *a clock* I'm checking?

The Mystery of the Japanese Clock

The *only* exceptions to chaos are good old thirty-four—but this time nineteen seconds long instead of sixteen or seventeen—and, in a way, the sixtieth or 00 second, seven seconds short, as I'd said it "always" was, and not the five seconds short it turned out to be in table one.

And then, the "miracle," which (I'll let you in on it) I'd been banking on. This welter of sixty minutes, which had left me aghast, adds up to an hour of exactly thirty-six hundred seconds.

That's much too good, was my first reaction. Much better if it were one or two seconds short or long. In fact, it's downright suspicious. That's the kind of result you get when the cheating scientist fakes it too well. I repeated the addition by calculator and by the method of adding sequentially "over" and "under sixties" in my head—and by subtotalling ten groups of six each and then adding the totals. It didn't change the result.

Well, I told myself, if my subconscious is so good it can pick a mess of sixty numbers near to sixty that nevertheless add up to thirty six hundred exactly, and then make my eyes see those sixty crazy numbers in succession, well, that will certainly be a mystery for someone to investigate. I promise you I'll keep my eyes peeled for any signs of such a wild talent in myself.

Want some "final explanations" and/or comments? Well, it seems to me, that with the clock's basic arrangement of cardboard or thin plastic panels stacked and slightly fanned out around a wheel, there'd always be a little play between them, slight changes in the way they fall and land and restack themselves for the next round between a panel and its neighbors, amounting to a different "shuffle" for each round, so they never fall quite the same way twice. To observe just how all this happens you'd need to get microscopic to find out.

But all this does not affect the revolving wheels and the time they take to make their rotations. The accuracy is in them and the panels have to reflect it in the long run, if not individually, then all together.

Over the past few days of my re-intensified interest in my Japanese clock I've been able to get as many as twenty readings on the time of the fall of the hour panel as measured against my Casio electronic watch, simply because the first makes an easily audible click and the latter announces each hour with ee [*sic—three?*] short beeps followed by one long one on the exact moment, so that I hear the latter and am able to watch seconds until I hear the former, without having to catch the panel's fall from the corner of my eye. The delay was always between 16 and 19 seconds. I imagine that like repeated observations of any individual minute-panel's fall would give similar results. I also think that if I'd still been timing the panel falls by wristwatch and run into small variations like these, I'd have ignored them and said the clock's time wasn't varying at all.

Another significant point: When I finished my second hour run-through, although I was eager to relax in relief and also to get the minute-length figures and check them against the three-year-earlier run-through, I also was conscious of a strong urge simply to keep on observing and recording the time of panel falls for another hour, to get a line on how many and how great changes I'd find from one hour to the next.

This of course is one line any "further research" on my Japanese clock would take—if I could bring myself to contemplate such obsessive madness. Two runs would be nothing in such research; I'd do dozens and dozens. Would I find there was a complete "reshuffle" each time, or would I discover *trends* in the delays or early-falls of each panel? Reluctantly (but with *great* relief) I renounce the project. I have a hunch I'd end up speculating about the effect on individual panel-falls of the vibrations from passing trucks (I'm on a busy downtown street) or earthquakes less than Richter-3 (I'm in San Francisco). That way, truly, for me at least, madness lies.

Or, *re* that "further research," I could, of course, go into the clock, take it apart, "pluck out the heart of its mystery," but that's always been against the rules of the little game I've been playing here, in which the clock's been a "black box" one may not open.

Or I could try to get hold of other clocks of the same model and test out those—no end to the directions an obsessive fascination could take.

But I am content—and I feel rather safer!—to end here.

QUICKS AROUND THE ZODIAC
—A Farce

THE SACRED SEASON nighs, and so Mother Dad Quick (that's me, dears—Mumsie) narrates another yearly installment in the saga of the Quick Family. As Guh-Gramps Quick likes to say, "There are only two kinds of critters in this universe: the Deads and the Quicks!"

Our Holy Babe, Daughter Estralita Quick, just floated out of our own private transporter room, rosy-fresh from her toddling class at our suburban swarm's one-grav gym, and lisped, "I'm Thanta Thlawth. Wanna prethent?" Whereat she puckered her cherubic lips and spitted at Mumsie's face a jet of cranberry juice to drop stickily down my personal privacy field inches in front of my eyes. The little rogue!

I indite this missive of good cheer from our new ranch-type satellite in the Second Circum-Polar Orbiting Volume, zoned only last Capricorn for suburban family dwellings, Dad's influence turning the tide. And I'm typing it with my own ten pinkies like an ancient stenographer—can't voice-write for three whole days, as my glottis is immobilized to allow a quick buff-job on my vocal cords to take. (Hold on to your hearts, you men, at our Xmas-Do, when you hear a 14-year-old sexpot

267

murmur slurpily behind you as she inserts a warm hand under your shirt!)

And so without more ado, I turn memory's pages back a full twelve months and begin the detailed tale of a wondrous and horrendous year that's left me speechless. (Ha-ha!) I use the true astrologic names of the months, as ordained by our beloved Church of Jesus Christ Spacegod, the swingingest sect in Christendom!

Aquarius (It's raining soup!): Son-in-Law Dirk Hunter's new pornflick "Space Chicks" premiered on Rigel Kentaurus IV (Far Centaurus Alpha!). Same night, by happy chance, Daughter Dorcas Quick Hunter popped, making me a host-grandmother. List to the tangled tale!—Nine months before, our ever-sensitive Dirk empathized so strongly with his femme ET co-star that they had a little interspecial accident. When "Chicks" finished shooting, the co-stars transported home in a big hurry to lay their troubles before Dorcas. After wifely demurs, her big heart got the better of her and she agreed to host the accident, so its authors could continue without break, or lawsuit, in that goldiferous moom pix biz! The blood-protein exchanges were a breeze for Dorcas and the transplant took on first try. Nine months later, on Aqua 7, Chickie emerged, born with a full suit of pink feathers, no less! (Dorcas said they'd been tickling for the last three months.) Soon the wee one was gayly cheeping and giddily wobble-flying in our home's free fall. Chickie Quick at once became the family favorite. (But Dorcas called her Quickie, for Dirk's boo-boo.)

Meanwhile I was immobilized a whole week getting a full bod newskinning. Afterwards I had to double my time in my space-karate class to get back in trim. Son Job Quick was off to Venus to enjoy the thrills of planet-dropping with his college chums. Daughter Cheri Quick, our stormy 12-year-old, won her highschool (500 miles high, ha-ha!) award for belly dancing, though how she does it with that flat tum I'd like to know. Daughter Estralita Quick went into Advanced Baby Talk two months ahead of her class.

At month's end, Dad Quick was off with his newsteam to survey Beta Ceti VI for investment and tax write-off purposes, stopping at Tau Ceti III to host a banquet, where he received his award as Entrepreneur of the Year. While I transported to a satellite of Circumluna to co-chair a retreat of the J. C. Stargod Matrons—"stargoddesses." May His cheery calm which saw him through his multicrucifixion on all planets and in all continua simultaneously enswirl you!

Pisces (We're in the soup, with the other fishes!): I returned from my space-do to find Son Job back from Venus and in the intensive care volume of our suburban swarm's orbiting hospital. He was in good spirits, but one-third covered with third-degree burns. He noted my newskin job (bod like inside fresh peapod) and said wistfully, "Mumsie, I wish they'd left one wrinkle." The old sentimentalist!

Next morning, Fluffy the cat had eaten Chickie! Quicks plunged in deepest gloom. Estralita disconsolate. "Chickie, come fly with me. Where are 'ou?" The Bureau of ET Welfare (Department of ET Affairs), Homicide, and the Transporting Squad were on our necks for a full ten days—and the SPCA. Fluffy banished to airlock.

Meanwhile the IRS arrived looking for Dad. "Just a routine checkout, Miz Quick"—I know those. They departed, leaving bugs in his study and our transporter room—secretly, they thought, but the Quicks are quicker. Her highschool reported Daughter Cheri failing in Meditation and Deportment—our dear activist! I doubled family prayer sessions. When all else fails, turn to J.C.S.!

Aries (We get butted, rammed with new realities.): At month's start Son-in-Law Dirk paid us a surprise visit from where he works "amidst the alien porn," as he puts it. With him came his lovely new co-star in hardcore spaceflick "Writhing Limbs," a charming ET femme with two arms and two legs like any normal person, except when she wants them to, they can unstiffen and make like snakes, most artistically. I thought her truly seductive, in suave international fashion. *Tres chic.* Well, it turned out Dirk's sensitivity (matched by hers) had betrayed him again. "Just one more first-of-the-month bill to pay, Mumsie," he quipped. Daughter Dorcas was naturally hesitant, but on our urgings soon came around— as I pointed out, it would be the best therapy for her, take her mind off Chickie. Her blood proteins were changed in a flash and the implant took like chickenpox! Before transporting back to location with his much-relieved snakegirl, Dirk joshed me, "Gee, Mumsie, I don't know why I keep chasing after those ET chicks when I could be back at Terra, balling you." I told him, "I know. Money." He said, eyeing me in my hostess bikini, "Right, Mumsie! Just the same, that newskin job is fab. I bet the only wrinkle they've left you on your bod is your snatch!" What a droll charmer, naively outspoken, our sweet Son-in-Law the space stud.

Daughter Cheri tops in Meditation, but schoolqueried about all—out sexing-the precocious slyboots! Son Job was brought home from intensive care, having astounded the crack medicos by his swift healing. The Quick blood. He seemed a little moody, but Mumsie'd soon see to that, I told myself. Daughter Estra suited up (how like her Doctor Dentons!) and jetted out to sell her first J. C. Stargod cookies to the neighbors. Fluffy out of airlock on good behavior. Dad back from Tau Ceti. Just in time to hear my tale of woe and say "Don't worry, Sleekie," then he was off to Fomalhaut. The Quicks do get around!

Taurus (We face the horns, are tossed afar.): This month (April Oldstyle) we celebrated as always our big ancestral event of the year: Guh-Gramps Quick's birthday party in the Cryogenic Vivarium of Perpetual Rest that orbits Neptune in the coolth of space. Son Job transported with us on his minibed. Soon we were part of the Quickswarm (a veritable ocutuple quincunx of Quicks) mingling eagerly await in a grand party ballroom of the Cry-Viva. By a matter-transmit mixup, Aunt Mitzie Quick Sappersteen arrived with the hands and forearms of a weight-lifter from Transylvania. "Like Popeye," said Cousin Dan Quick, a comics buff.

Then in no time at all, or so it seemed, Guh-Gramps was whipped from zero Kelv to normal temp. He looked around with grim approval, "counting the house." He was much taken with Son Job in his minibed and returned to him more than once to ask his health. He said to Daughter Dorcas, "You look peaked." (He thought I was her younger sister, a natural mistake.) He shook us each by the hand as we paddled past. Aunt Mitzie squeezed a bit too hard (no wonder!) and there was a flutter of nurses. But at last Guh-Gramps smiled and said to all (we hushed): "You know, folks, there are only two kinds of critters in this universe, the Deads and the Quicks!" We all laughed heartily and then made merry, but after that high point Guh-Gramps seemed to become more and more uneasy. Even going through the year's obits didn't cheer him much. Soon he was saying, "Well, so long, folks, see you next year," and while the dissipatory neutrino field returned him ;o zero Kelv (or near) we all sang "Happy Birthday" ending with the traditional "Keep coming back. Don't go away," which somehow struck an eerie note.

We all transported home, Ms. Soi Sappersteen (Aunt Mitz) to Lost and Found.

Gemini (Crickets! Each trouble has a lovely twin— Serenity.): We launched Daughter Cheri on a hormone course to bud her breasts, so she can have her agecome this year. (That's her barmitzvah, Uncle Sol.) While she's still twelve, not unlucky thirteen. Son Job left his minibed, flabby from skingraft surgery, so joined me in karate drill, upon persuasion. After the third session (quite stiff) he confided wistfully, "You know, Mumsie, I sometimes wish you were, well, sort of *frail* and that you did something like, well, knitting, instead of martial arts." I laughed indulgently. What's a boy's mother for, if not to provide a high example of vibrant allaround womanhood? "Why did you name me Job?" he next inquired. "The numerologist—" I began. "Never mind," he said. "It suits." My serious one!

Daughter Dorcas began to complain of morning sickness and of Babe Estralita's prattle. (She's got a new game with Fluffy: "Who ate Chickie?") I sent the one to bed, the other to weekend catch up class. And prayed to J.C.S.—it always helps.

During an umbra hour, Dad sneaked home, having won fresh honors on Formalhaut V. He had to find some very important papers, to destroy. As we emerged from shadow, the IRS arrived, looking for him—five minutes after he'd left for Altair IV.

Cancer (We don't quite get it, this time around.): For openers, catastrophe! Dad's program off the air, no warning. Pub serv "Camping on Titan" replaced. "News Leaks" said, "Last hour 'Hot Planets,' investment-tips frontrunner, was dark-first cancellation of Quinn Quick's brainchild since Pleiades uraniumfields washout." That night Gig Ellis (You know him, folks—Dad's best friend and my old flame) brought word from Dad: "No change vacation plans." Nothing but that! Mumsie threw a tantrum ornamented with karate figures. But Gig saw me through it—so sweet. That man should be in pornflicks! Later that night Son Job left for practice mountain-climb in Kansas with college chums. Surprised, I queried, "What's wrong with karate?" He said passively, "It's too personal. I want solitude." Our poet. Daughter Cheri was elected Junior Spacepod Queen. At J. C. Stargod regional do, I led prayers for Saint Daniken, hardly impeded by my pucker-lips operation. (Watch out, you men!)

Leo (We walk about as roaring lions, devouring fun.): Surmounting initial difficulties, the entire Dad Quinn Quick family enjoyed a grand vacation at Disneyland on Delta Dorado III "amongst the Southern Stars" (really quite as familiar to us as the northern because of our home's circumpolar orbit). I had to do a last-minute transport to Kansas to collar Son Job off of a plastic mock-up of Mount Everest (really quite aweinspiring). Daughter Dorcas wanted to beg off because of her delicate condition, but I charmed her out of her fears. Doglegging in from Canopus IX, Dad joined us on the way at Achernar IV, where we had to transfer on our matter-transmit route.

Dorado Disneyland was sheer delight. You'd think you were in Southern California. Estralita got sick on authentic cotton candy. You'd never guess our welcoming committee when we got home—the IRS. But Dad Quick (clever man!)

had split for survey in the Southern Cross. Son Job hied back to Kansas.

Virgo (The best virginity is a virgin mind.): Daughter Cheri starred at her agecome. Truly, that girl has genuine acting talent. When she said, "Now I am a woman," I cried unashamedly. A host of female relatives, including Aunt Mitz with (wouldn't you know it?) the torso and purple-flowered hostess gown of a lady from Spokane she'd been talking to at the transfer station. After the ceremony Estralita, who'd been Cheri's flowergirl, said mischievously, "Mumsie, can I 'tart fucking now?" The little devil!

The subsequent festivities were briefly interrupted when they brought Job home. He was in good spirits, but had broken his neck in a fall on a plastic mock-up of the Matterhorn. Careful handling, excellent medical help, many prayers, and he made a marvelous recovery—but I anticipate. We ended up the happy do with a round of toasts, squeezed from our little monogrammed cocktail bags, Job watching from his minibed. Until you've seen an agecome in free fall, you've seen nothing. All wished much happiness to our lovely agecomer, who looked positively radiant in her formal peekaboo gown. Her little breasts had budded to perfection. "Oh, Mumsie, I'm exploding!" she confided. Then all dispersed to their homes, Aunt Mitz to Lost and Found once more, poor mix-prone dear.

Libra (We are weighed in the balance and found having. Ah, there's such wisdom in astrology!): "Hot Tentacles of Love" (new title "Writhing Limbs") sneakpreviewed Beta Arietis VI. Same fine morning Daughter Dorcas announced dramatically, "I feel it wriggling!" Meanwhile Son-in-Law Dirk had started work in "Space Pussies." Holy cats! On some planet or other of Deneb, the one in Delphinus, or maybe Capricorn. (How life and astrology interweave! It's quite remarkable. Inscrutable wisdom of J. C. Stargod, Bless Him!) Dirk's new smutfilm caught the imagination of my youngest daughters. Estralita told Fluffy, "You hear dat, puddy tat? Gonna be in t'ree-dee sexies." While Cheri announced, "Mumsie, I know what I want to be—a pornstar!" "You'd have to start with bit parts," I reminded her. "I know that, Mumsie-bratty little sisters. But they help get the hero worked up." "Why not send Dirk a stat then?" I suggested, always practical.

Scorpio (We scuttle about, get painfully stung.): Dad Quinn Quick returned home in triumph from a big financial news scoop in Musca, near Crux, in time to host with me our bidecennial groupie reunioncompanions of *our* happy high-school days. Jean, Joan, Georgina, Georgie, Gig—everyone! And all, bar none, vastly successful since. Aunt Mitz came as observer, unmixed for a wonder. Daughter Cheri remembered to send us greetings, although she was in the middle of her agecome saturnalia on Eros (pleasure satellite of Venus, not asteroid)—such a thoughtful girl! Son Job looked on from his minibed, quite glum, poor dear, and with stiffly fixed gaze (his healing neck). Estralita felt left out, started to cry. "Oh, Mumsie, what's for *me*?" But Cousin Dan Quick (he's actually in our group, a kissing cousin) stopped her tears with the inspired gift of a rare old comic book "The Myth of Cthulhu." (How strangely they spelled names in those old days.)

Then when the festivities were at their height (I was in a *Halasana*, would you believe it?) disaster struck in the form of an IRS arresting team, which without ceremony plucked Dad from our daisy chain and hustled him off to jail-quite brutally, ripping off his wrist phone, though not before he got in a call to his lawyers. What a gloomy mishap! Gig had his work cut out for him, consoling me.

Sagittarius (We shoot our arrows everywhere and where they fall we do not care. Surprised to hear I just sold a poem to "Your Lucky Stars"? First in a series.): Son Job astounded us all by enlisting in the Space Marines the day he came of military age. "You're choosing martial arts?" I asked him in surprise, I couldn't help it. "I thought you wanted solitude?" "Yes, and I'll get it," he told me, nodding grimly (his neck's quite healed). I didn't know then that their new boot camp is on Pluto.

When no word came from Dad for two whole weeks, even by way of his expensive lawyers, I brought the Civil Liberties Union into it *and* the Bureau of ET Welfare. I sat down (their offices have grav) and proved to them that Dad was legally an ET. During the past five years he's spent nine-tenths of his time off earth and amongst them, which is the common requirement for being able to incorporate businesses in your own name but as an ET under other jurisdictions than Terra's. They really looked surprised at first, but then most interested.

Next day I discovered Daughter Dorcas reading Malfort's *Space Beasts*. "Just take a look at this," she said direly. "It seems that on Snakegirl's planet, eight tentacles are normal (and sixteen a blessing) but that those born with only four are considered hideously deformed and are forced to seek employment off planet. However—get this!—such cripples invariably breed true in the next generation, and their nor-mat offspring are welcomed back."

"Well," I said reasonably, "at least that means the child will always have a place to go if she doesn't fit in here." 1 was also thinking how fortunate it was that Snakegirl had found the pornflicks to work in. The ways of J. C. Stargod are mysterious,

but always helpful if you hunt deep enough. However, I forbore
to mention that to Daughter Dorcas. I could hardly expect
her to worry about Snakegirl's plight when she was in *her*
condition, which by now had become quite obvious.

"Oh, Mumsie," Dorcas said, slamming the book shut and
wincing—she must have felt a big wriggle, but I forbore to ask.
She said, "Will you at least keep that 'Lita brat of yours from bug-
ging me? She's always following me around these days, staring
at my abdomen and asking me embarrassing questions."

True enough, my youngest was peering big-eyed, from
where she was floating, through the arms of the whatnot,
to which we pin all sorts of objects in free fall. Fluffy was in
her arms. It seemed to me perfectly natural—indeed, most
healthy—that she should be deeply interested in her oldest
sister's host-pregnancy, but I knew Dorcas was in no mood to
be reasonable. I swam toward the kitchen, scooping up the
wee ones on the way. "Come, dear," I told 'Lita. "Dorkie's
not feeling well. We'll meditate and I'll give you a chocolate
cookie." "And one for Thoo-loo too?" she coaxed.

(She's brought this ancient comics character Cthulhu
into the Chickie games she plays with Fluffy. This Thoo-loo
is like a frog, but has wings and claws and tentacles—quite
picturesque.) In the kitchen we found Cheri pensively ingest-
ing milk—she'd returned from Eros with dark circles under her
coral eyes (new contact lenses, same tint as her nipples) but
otherwise her dauntless self.

Capricorn (Who's the goat this time, one or all of us?):
And now we're in the Holy Month, and the Yuledo draws nigh.
(If your stat's starred, you're invited.) And I can't speak to you
(my glottis job, remember?) but I can still type out our joys
and woes, which never end. (My ten pinkies—recall?—which

have been compared to the thistledown-shod shoon of elves. Under the moon in silver shoon, tra-la!)

Dad's lawyers called, gently reproving me for dragging in the ET Welfare Bureau (I bet it saved their necks!) and then coyly revealing Dad will be home for Xmas (I did that)! His case comes up in six months, by which time he'll be in Andromeda, I have no doubt. (Intergalactic flight is on the brink.)

Early this month Dirk statted us that he'll be home for Xmas too! Deneb IV (it's the one in Delphinus) is a dismal planet 'way out in the sticks,' he says, and "Space Pussies" a drag except for his new ET femme co-star, who's home-sick too—"my Lonely Leopardess," he calls her. "He sounds like he's getting sensitive again," Dorcas said glumly. He says he can't wait until he's back orbiting Terra and hugging his three really-truly girl friends under the mistletoe. "Who's the third he means?" Dorcas asked. "Cheri now or the Lonely Leopardess? Oh well."

Which brings me to a bit of wondrous news. Dirk's stat held detailed directions for Cheri. She followed them and after grueling screen tests which she passed with flying colors (coral and turquoise green—for her new hairdo) she has unprecedentedly been selected for (hold onto your seats, folks) *the fourth femme lead* in the new terrapornflick "Barmitzvah Belles!" (Don't fight it, Uncle Sol.)

Amidst these joys, a spot of dreadful tragedy, of course. His second day in boot camp, Job deep-froze in a wink "due to a malfunction of his thermal suit," the Govt stat said. They also sent a pic to reassure us. He was smiling, as if in good spirits, but rather fixedly, also quite pale, being near zero Kelv. He's being transported to the trans-neptunian Cry-Viva (he'll be with GuhGramps!) and warmed by slow degrees "with tender loving care." I'll bet he gets a crush on some nice pretty nurse and doesn't even think to screw her—my preoccupied innocent! With any luck he'll be home for Xmas too.

Just now Daughter Dorcas hurtled in, pursued by Estralita. The Terrible Tot, our precious, wove around our host-mother as if she were a maypole, waving at her abdomen and chanting tunefully, "Yoo-hoo, Thoo-loo! We love you-loo!"

Which somehow sums up the seasonal sentiments of the entire Dad Quick Family, it suddenly seems to me. The Yule Babe comes…to Bethlehem…and us!

So so long, folks! See you on Xmas—if your stat is starred. Or call us up Xmas Eve. Our phone is panoramic, so you can see the whole damn family—the whole two-day party if you want. But watch that phone bill! But don't expect me. I begin to have a feeling I'll be tired.